PRAISE FOR *BLOOM*:

"A cottagecore dream turned nightmare, astonishing in its beauty and violence. Every page drips with delicious dread. This bite-sized tale is perfectly wicked."
RACHEL HARRISON, author of *Such Sharp Teeth*

"Sumptuous, lyrical prose meets horrific brutality in Delilah S. Dawson's harrowing tale of obsession and cruelty. An elegantly written nightmare, *Bloom* will beguile unsuspecting readers before finally slicing deep and drawing blood."
ERIC LaROCCA, author of *Things Have Gotten Worse Since We Last Spoke*

"Dawson has brought the kind of irresistible treat you've been hungering for. Sapphic longing with a dash of darkness — the perfect recipe. Superbly seductive."
HAILEY PIPER, author of *A Light Most Hateful*

"Sensual, smart, biting, and downright nasty, *Bloom* is a dizzying, heady feast for the discerning palate. I devoured this book in one greedy sitting."
PAUL TREMBLAY, author of *The Pallbearers Club*

"Delicate and murderous, *Bloom* is the perfect encapsulation of a subgenre I'd only heard of in theory but now exists in its final form: cozy horror. Delight in the berries, blood and cupcake frosting — find yourself enraptured by the farmers' market aesthetic as designed by the Mads Mikkelson version of Hannibal Lecter."
CHUCK WENDIG, author of *The Book of Accidents*

"Like an unwary visitor to the Goblin Market, I was swept away by Delilah S. Dawson's *Bloom*, with its lush cottagegore settings and heart of absolute darkness."
ALLY WILKES, author of *All the White Spaces*

"Gruesome and lovely, *Bloom* is compulsively readable. Like being slowly boiled alive, by the time you see the rot beneath the beauty, it's already too late. You're hooked."
KRISTI DeMEESTER, author of *Such a Pretty Smile*

BLOOM

Also by Delilah S. Dawson

The Violence

THE BLUD SERIES
Wicked as They Come
Wicked As She Wants
Wicked After Midnight
Wicked Ever After

THE HIT SERIES
Hit
Strike

Servants of the Storm
Midnight at the Houdini

Mine
Camp Scare

Star Wars: Phasma
Star Wars Galaxy's Edge: Black Spire
Star Wars Inquisitor: Rise of the Red Blade
Disney Mirrorverse: Pure of Heart
The Minecraft Mob Squad Series

THE SHADOW SERIES,
WRITTEN AS LILA BOWEN
Wake of Vultures
Conspiracy of Ravens
Malice of Crows
Treason of Hawks

BLOOM

DELILAH S.
DAWSON

TITAN BOOKS

Bloom

Print edition ISBN: 9781803365756

E-book edition ISBN: 9781803365763

Published by Titan Books

A division of Titan Publishing Group Ltd

144 Southwark Street, London SE1 0UP

www.titanbooks.com

First edition: October 2023

10 9 8 7 6 5 4 3 2 1

A CIP catalogue record for this title is available from the British Library.

Printed and bound by CPI Group (UK) Ltd, Croydon CR0 4YY.

For my beloved daughter Rhys, a brilliant
artist and baker, who requested it.

Thank you for the inspiration.
And the cupcakes.

1

The modern world is severely lacking in magic, and those who crave it are at a constant disadvantage because they are desperate and it's in short supply. Some places — amusement parks, country fairs, museums, old bookstores — can temporarily fill the void, but there will always be people who check every armoire for a door to Narnia, every rabbit hole for a road to Wonderland. One such person is Ro, born Rosemary Dutton, age twenty-seven, whose life imploded last year, leaving her an absolute wreck.

Ro has spent so much time deconstructing the great works of literature that she has completely failed to live an adventure of her own. Now, finally finished with her PhD at Columbia, and having published her thesis in book form with a small press and secured an assistant professorship at the University of Georgia, she is trying to create her own everyday magic. That's why she has come to the farmers' market enlivening the tree-lined park just off campus. There is a certain sorcery to such a market: rows of stalls and tents filled with homemade cinnamon buns, leggy tomato plants, bear-shaped jars of wildflower honey, vegetables still dusted with dirt, rosy peaches with raindrops trapped in their fur.

This is Ro's first visit, and she can feel the glitter in the air. This place feels like *Stardust* and *A Midsummer Night's Dream* and *Labyrinth* had an orgy and popped out a slightly bougie baby behind a baseball field. Sure, there was a cute market near Books of Wonder back in the city, but there's something otherworldly about this place, with the sun filtering through ancient oaks and butterflies billowing through the crowd. Ro is the kind of optimist who was disappointed to discover that the only alchemy behind the hedonistic glory of a handcrafted Starbucks frappé is three pumps of mass-produced sugar syrup, and she suspects that things here are more genuine somehow.

So far, she has a pint of strawberries, a loaf of bread, and a log of cheese made from the milk of a goat named Belinda, according to the label. She's been in town only half a year and hasn't made any friends yet, and is definitely not ready to date again, but this market makes her feel like she's out in the world, doing things, hoping kismet will come calling. Most of the time, she is happy to vacillate between home and classroom, feverishly researching her next book and striving for a good word from her department head even though it's only her second semester. She can get annoyingly hermetic and obsessive about her work, but this charming bazaar is making her feel like destiny is right around the corner. Right here, right now, she wants to be the kind of woman who carries a jute tote bag as the summer breeze blows through her long, loose hair, the kind of woman who knows exactly what to wear and where to go and what to say. She has always longed to be effortless — effortlessly cool, effortlessly confident, effortlessly thin.

That last one definitely never came to pass. She thinks of herself as curvy on a good day, chubby on a bad day. Most days, she's somewhere in between, feeling doomed to a body that isn't what she would choose, like she accidentally stepped into the wrong dress and now can't get it unzipped.

As it turns out, it takes a lot of effort to seem effortless. It takes patience, which is not her bailiwick, plus a sense of preternatural chill that she has never possessed. Ro would like to be breezy, but she seems to swing between periods of dedicated, obsessive effort and slothlike, stubborn inertia. She'd like to think her unpredictability is quirky, but in their big, final fight, Erik called it impossible.

Erik said a lot of things then, most of them cruel.

Ro is still recovering.

He would hate this farmers' market. Would call it pedestrian and tedious. Would poke fun at Ro's attempt to blend into this colorful suburban college town when he craves the sharp, shiny sophistication of New York. But it doesn't matter what Erik would think, because after three years of dating, one day Ro found a pink lady's razor and a small box of tampons hidden in the back of his bathroom cabinet, did a little digging around in his iPad, and discovered he preferred the sharp, shiny hipbones of one of his sophomore honors students.

Well, she'll take a sleepy Saturday in the sunshine over getting negged by the guy who broke her heart any day. Her mother cried when she found out they'd split, bemoaning the wedding bells she was now certain would never ring for her weird, studious daughter. There are no rich men in academia, her mother told her when she was filling out college applications. Better to get a bachelor's degree in something money-adjacent and snag a man with a trust fund. Ro's middle-class dad never reached his potential in sales and then died at fifty, leaving two mortgages, and Ro knows her expected duty as an only child was to marry well and provide a comfortable retirement for her mother back home in Savannah.

Oops.

Her mother kept trying to set her up with the divorced older sons of her church friends, and during their last fight they both said things that can't be unsaid.

And so here she is: single, employed, and with her mom blocked on her phone. No contact with Erik or her last close relative. They both warned her she'd be lonely, and she is, but in a good way. She doesn't hate it here, but she misses New York and fully believes that's where she'll end up long term, once she has a few years of teaching under her belt.

The market is unexpectedly crowded, with dozens of people lined up outside of a taco truck wedged in between the white plastic tents. As Ro considers whether or not buying macarons is worth having to talk to the Ms. Frizzle wannabe selling them, there's a loud thump and a screech. A somethingdoodle the color of toast breaks free of the thickest part of the crowd and darts past Ro with a stolen sausage in its mouth. She lurches back, tripping over a knee-high boy wearing a monkey backpack with a leash attached to it.

"I'm so sorry," she says to the harried mother, who snatches up her crying spawn like Ro tried to kidnap him.

"You need to be more careful," the mother says before shaking her head and towing her child away.

Ro watches them go, slightly baffled by the fact that the offended mom was about her age. She still feels seventeen inside, not nearly old enough to be responsible for anything needier than her cat. How do other people already have things figured out? Until now, Ro has lived for her grades and her work and, much to her dismay, Erik. She's not sure what comes next.

She feels eyes on her, a soft and curious prickle like moth feet, and she turns to find the most beautiful girl in the world staring at her. While attempting not to flatten a child, Ro has somehow managed to stumble into a stall she hasn't seen before, and the girl behind the counter looks like a goddamn elf, like the apotheosis of cottagecore, like if a Studio Ghibli heroine could be a pale white girl with long hair as tawny and true as corn silk. On the table before her are bars of soap in delicate pastel colors, sprinkle-spackled cupcakes stacked on scalloped stands, butter-gold beeswax candles, jelly jars of honey with thick blocks of comb and gingham tops tied with ribbons. The sides of her stand feature wooden shelves crowded with glossy green plants in grower pots — plants with round leaves like lily pads and pointy leaves like puppet tongues and wide, veiny leaves like elephant ears. Ro doesn't know their names, but she's seen them on Instagram.

"See anything you like?" the girl says with a knowing smile.

For a moment, Ro can only stare at her, taking in the details of her ice-blue eyes and her constellation of freckles and her perfect, tiny teeth and the creamy skin revealed by the low-cut neck of her dress, which is lavender and long and airy and looks homemade, exactly like the sort of thing that should be worn right before someone is abducted to Faerie.

Ro doesn't know what to say. Words are her world, and yet she is speechless. This happens sometimes. She understands books so much better than she understands people. That's why she writes non-fiction, and that's why she has trouble making friends and has mostly dated very nerdy guys who share her esoteric literary interests.

Before this moment, she was fairly certain she was straight, but now she is thrown into utter chaos.

"What flavor are the cupcakes?" she asks, deflecting.

The girl — because yes, of course she is a woman, and yet there is something uniquely fresh and innocent about her — points with a long, graceful finger. "Lavender, lemon, strawberry, vanilla. All the chocolate are gone, I'm afraid."

"Do you make them yourself?" Because yes, yes, the more questions she asks, the more the girl has to answer and the longer Ro can stand here being mesmerized. She briefly wonders if eating the girl's food is anything like Persephone slipping rose-red seeds between her lips in the Underworld.

"I do. It's my grandmother's recipe — well, the base recipe, at least. I like to experiment with frosting flavors." She points to a dainty porcelain tray loaded with samples of cake, each bite-sized cylinder tufted with frosting. "Try one, if you like. The cupcakes are four dollars each or four for fifteen."

Ro plucks one of the lavender samples and pops it in her mouth, painfully aware that the girl is watching her with sharp eyes. Flavor explodes on her palate — she's never tasted frosting this silky before. She rubs it between her tongue and the roof of her mouth, luxuriating in it. Their eyes meet with an electric shock, and she feels *seen*, she feels *known*. She feels *magic*.

"Good God," she murmurs as she chews. "That's the most flawlessly unctuous thing I've ever tasted."

The girl's eyes brighten, and she smiles like a cat — she has a crooked canine.

Ro wants to lick it.

And she doesn't know what to do with that information.

She swallows and wipes the crumbs from her lips, annoyed because she knows the hunter-green polish on her nails is chipped and that the girl has definitely noticed. Ro thinks of herself as a cozy mess. This girl is precise, polished, and practically perfect.

"Unctuous," the girl says as if tasting the word for the first time.

"In the best possible way," Ro assures her. "Can I get a lavender, please?"

The girl nods and takes a moment, as if trying to select the best possible lavender cupcake, before presenting Ro with a square white box. Ro holds the box stupidly for a moment before remembering that this is an exchange. She has to set it down on the table to dig for her wallet, and only then does she remember she has no cash.

"Do you take cards? Because if not, I might have to work it off washing dishes or something." She feels her cheeks go red as the traitorous words rush out of her mouth. When her dad used to say this at Outback Steakhouse, it was accepted as a dad joke. When she says it to the girl at the farmers' market, it sounds to her like a proposition.

The girl holds out an iPad with a Square attached. "I take cards."

Ro gives the girl her card.

"Rosemary Dutton," the girl muses before sliding the card through and handing it back. "There's rosemary, that's for remembrance."

"I go by Ro." She always has to say this, short and sharp, every time something becomes official.

The girl hands her card back. "You shouldn't."

"I'm more of a Ro. I don't like Rosemary."

"You can be anything you want to be. And I think Rosemary is a beautiful name."

There's a challenge in the girl's eyes, and she makes Ro want to want to be Rosemary, for all that she doesn't know how and has flinched at her proper name since she was little. It does not escape her that the girl has just quoted Shakespeare at her, which is practically foreplay to a literary scholar.

"What's your name?" she asks, turning the challenge around.

"Ash."

"Not Ashley?" she teases.

A smirk. "Not Ashley."

They stand there, and Ro realizes that she has her card back and her cupcake in hand and no reason to keep standing here, smiling like a loon.

"Can I get you anything else?" Ash finally asks.

Your number. Your story. The scratch of your nails against my scalp.

"This should do it. Thanks." Ro gives a little wave and leaves. Never has she been so aware of walking away. Do women watch for the same things men do, she wonders? Do they like the swing of hips, the bounce of butts, the sway of long hair?

Does...does *she* like these things?

She is aware that for someone who has always considered herself to be straight, she still looks at girls' butts, but she always assumed this was because she was comparing herself, maintaining an inner rating system to see where she landed because that's how internalized misogyny works. Now she wonders if maybe she looks for another reason.

She is still carrying her debit card in one hand like an absolute idiot.

Once she's out of range, she stops and puts away her card and places the cupcake carefully in her jute bag. She's only seen half of the market stalls, but she can't imagine that anything else might compare to the small, peculiar magic of what she's just experienced. There is Disney World, and then there is the speed bump in her neighborhood, and only one makes her want to return again and again.

She heads for her car and checks herself out in the mirror. Same honey-blonde hair, long and wavy. Same warm brown eyes. And yet something has fundamentally changed.

She is thinking of ice-blue eyes and freckles, of hair as fine as silk.

When she gets home, she eats her cupcake with one of her grandmother's silver teaspoons. She savors every bite, rolling it around her mouth, luxuriously pushing frosting against her palate with her tongue. She thinks of Ash's finger, dipping in to taste the batter, making sure it's just right. On a college semester abroad, Ro once touched a painting by Van Gogh in an atelier somewhere in France, and she likes to think about how some of those atoms are still rattling around in her body.

Now the girl is like that, too: with her always, like magic.

That night, as she sips chardonnay and takes notes for her next book, her cat, Anon, vaults out of her lap and rushes to the nearest open window. As Ro rubs at the marks his claws have left on her thighs, he leaps to the sill and hisses through the screen, puffing up like a dandelion as he stares out into the night.

Ro stands and puts her notebook down before tiptoeing to the window. She peeks out but doesn't see or hear anything unusual outside in the heavily forested backyard. Still, there is some otherworldly feeling of being watched, of not being alone. Anon is still at full puff, glaring into the darkness. There must be an animal out there or something. She's never seen him behave this way before.

Shooing him off the windowsill, she closes the window and lowers the blinds all the way. Just to be safe, she checks the locks on both doors and closes the rest of the windows, cutting off the high-pitched hum of cicadas and the screams of horny tree frogs. It's been a change, falling asleep to nature instead of

Manhattan's constant din of honks and sirens. She's felt so safe here, by comparison. She'd thought Anon did, too.

"Oh, thou lily-livered boy," she says fondly.

She sits back down and takes up her pen, ignoring her cat's soft paws battering desperately at the glass.

2

It's Saturday and, like a junkie seeking a hit, Ro is back at the farmers' market. Last week, she wore the same sort of thing she would wear to the grocery store or to work: jeans, a nice tee, a blazer, light makeup, comfortable flats. Today, she spent an hour trying things on and throwing them back into her closet. She wants to look like what Ash would like, and this is an unusual feeling. She is not the sort of person who generally wants to please complete strangers.

She settled on a silky mauve shell and light jeans. She painted her toenails to match and wore espadrilles. She stared into her jewelry box, trying to remember if Ash was wearing any jewelry. She didn't think so. There was a simple elegance to her, a glowing plainness. She didn't need adornment. But does she like that sort of thing on other people?

There's the real question. Are women attracted to what they are themselves, or to something completely different? And why is it so confusing?

Ro settles on a dainty chain with a sunburst pendant. Someone who raises plants must like the sun, she reasons. As a student of literature, she often thinks in symbols.

The only flaw in her plan is the presence of looming gray clouds. In her mind, it's a beautiful blue day, and her luscious locks billow come-hitheringly in the wind. In reality, her hair is bouffy thanks to the humidity and she has to carry a bright pink umbrella that in no way matches her carefully chosen outfit.

The market isn't as popular today, thanks to the weather. There is no huge crowd outside the food truck, no loose dog causing serendipitous chaos, no tethered child of an outraged mother to stumble over. Ro reaches Ash's stall and chickens out twice before finally ducking inside. Ash is helping an elderly woman select a plant, calmly explaining the level of sunlight and amount of water it requires. Ro steps to the soap, lifting the samples to her nose and inhaling deeply. Vanilla, lavender, chamomile, oatmeal and honey, rose, sage. Each bar she touches evokes moods. She imagines a homey kitchen with a pie in the oven, silver shears cutting a thorny stem dotted with dew, summer sun filtered through a butterfly's wing. Everything in this booth means something else, layers to be unpeeled. All of it calls to her, shiny glints to a magpie.

"You're back." Ash appears at her side as the old woman leaves. She's wearing a sage-green dress today with her hair up in a braid crown, plus brown boots like something from *Anne of Green Gables*.

"I always come back for good cupcakes." Yes. Yes. That sounds suave.

"I'm glad. I made a batch special for you."

Ro's heart kicks up like the opening night of a play. Ash goes to her table and holds up a cupcake: plump, pretty, with a high swirl of butter-yellow frosting, crowned with a spiny green sprig. "Rosemary lemon." She holds it out — doesn't put it in a box or offer a bite-sized sample, just holds the cupcake out on her palm.

Uncertain, Ro takes it and swipes a dab of frosting off with a finger, popping it in her mouth. She is struck anew with the richness: fresh, bright lemon and the sharp, woody tang of rosemary. Ash is smiling at her expectantly.

"That's phenomenal. Frisson-worthy."

"Go on," Ash urges teasingly. "You have to try the cake with the frosting. It's a totality."

Ro gives a lopsided smile. "A conversation, not a monologue."

Okay, so Ro came here because she is drawn to Ash, but that doesn't mean she immediately understands her. Ash, so far, is a singular sort of mystery, an outlier, a new species she can't yet read. Ash feels like a test she doesn't know how to study for, a scene for which she hasn't memorized the lines. Is this a normal interaction between artisan and customer, two friendly female strangers, or is Ash flirting with her? Ro has never had a group of girlfriends — or even a best friend — not since Cecilia Looper turned on her in fifth grade. She has been part of a group in various drama clubs or grad-school study circles, but she hasn't spent much time one-on-one with a woman who wasn't her academic advisor. There is no clear path.

There is only a girl — a woman — about her age, ethereal and beautiful and strange, daring her to eat something too big, too messy. There are no napkins here, no forks. Whatever she does, she will look a fool.

Still, she'd rather be a fool on command than refuse and prove that she's dead inside — or, worse, that she's boring.

She peels back the brown wrapper and is about to take a bite right where the frosting and cake meet, but then she remembers an old gif she saw on Tumblr a thousand years ago. With a small grin of triumph, she gently pries the cake into two slabs and squeezes the frosting between them to make a sandwich before taking a more reasonable bite.

The satisfaction and awkwardness of the gesture are lost as she rolls the cupcake around her mouth, luxuriating in the sweet, the tart, the bready, the, *yes*, moist. A tiny moan escapes her lips, and she glances at Ash's face in time to see something bright flare behind her eyes, a small triumph of her own. Their eyes lock as she takes a second bite. She wants to keep tasting it. She wants to prolong the magic.

"The rosemary and lemons are from my garden," Ash says. "Picked fresh yesterday."

"Not to be repetitive, but it's incredible." Ro realizes she's going to devour the whole thing standing right here and instead wipes the crumbs from her lips. "There's something about the frosting. It's got a depth to it — "

"Lard. Most people use butter. I think it adds a certain something."

"It's a good thing I'm not a vegetarian."

Ash chuckles. "If you weren't supposed to eat meat, you wouldn't have canine teeth." She shows her teeth, but it's not a smile.

"I'll definitely take four of those," Ro says, because she isn't sure what else to say. "Or three, I guess, since I'm already halfway done with this one."

Ash smiles for real this time and goes behind the table, putting three of the cupcakes in a bigger box and tying it with a pink and white striped ribbon. "See anything else you need?"

Ro notices language, so she notices the different phrasing.

Anything you like.

Anything you *need*.

"Tell me about the soaps." Because she doesn't want to know which one smells better or is more moisturizing. She wants to know if Ash sees objects as stories the way she does.

Ash walks to the soap display and picks up a bar of the vanilla-bean soap. It's creamy white and flecked with dots of black that remind Ro of melting ice cream. Ash holds it lightly. Her nails are bare, cut short and scrubbed clean.

"Vanilla grows in hot, wet places. It's a climbing vine that produces a beautiful flower that blooms for only a day. If the right kind of bee comes along during that day, carrying exactly the right kind of pollen, you get vanilla beans. Society has decided that 'vanilla' means plain and boring, but it's actually quite rare and special. I grow it in my greenhouse. What you buy in the little brown jars at the store can't compare. Smell."

She waggles the bar of soap under Ro's nose, and it's as if she's smelling vanilla for the first time, or possibly inhaling the

Platonic ideal of vanilla after a lifetime of artificial flavoring. She can also smell the lightest waft of rose, which she assumes is from Ash's skin. Ash seems like the kind of person who would wish to smell of roses.

"I'll take that, too," she says softly, tamping down the urge to bite the soap.

Ash places the soap on the cupcake box. "Anything else? Plants?"

"I have a black thumb," Ro admits.

"No one can kill a snake plant."

"Try me. I don't mean to — I have the best intentions — but they die."

A chuckle. "You love them too much. You love them to death."

Ro cocks her head. "How so?"

"Snake plants thrive on neglect. They really only die if you water them too much. Hence, they die of love." Ash plucks a spiky-looking plant from the shelf. "I want you to take this plant home and neglect it. Put it by a bright window where the sun won't actually touch it and don't water it for a week. Not a drop."

Ash shoves the plant into Ro's hands like someone shoving a baby at a childless aunt. She has no choice but to accept it. She instantly pities it.

"I'm going to kill this plant," she warns.

"You won't. I won't let you. Bring me a picture of it next Saturday, and we'll see."

Ro's heart hiccups.

Next Saturday.

"I'll do my best to mistreat it, then," she says, wishing stabby plants weren't so awkward to hold. "What do I owe you?"

Ash glances around. "Ten for the cupcakes, five for the soap, five for the plant."

"I thought the cupcakes were four for fifteen…"

Ash's eyes go bright like a seagull spotting a kid with a corn dog. "You get friend prices."

They do the iPad dance and Ro knows she has to leave because there are two fourteen-year-old baby witches whispering while they wait for their turn. Being around Ash is like…like being bathed in moonlight. She shines, but in an entirely different way than the hot, punishing sun. There's a welcome coolness there, a quenching. Ro wants to roll belly-up and wriggle on her back in the grass.

"See you next week," Ro says.

Ash's eyes dance. "I hope so."

As she navigates the pitiful crowd, Ro doesn't stop for the bright red strawberries, the rosy peaches, the bright green ramps. She wants to get home and bathe with this soap, rubbing it into her skin in lazy circles. She wants to eat the rest of the cupcake in private, where no one can see the feelings it brings bubbling up. She wants to find a home for the plant and begin to lovingly neglect it.

When she gets to her car, there's a flyer under her windshield wiper. She stashes her jute bag in the front seat before pulling it out.

A girl has gone missing—a pretty girl with a pixie cut and glasses, a junior at the college. Milla Fairfax. Her mother is begging for any information regarding her whereabouts.

Girls disappear from college towns all the time, Ro thinks. Some, like her, have simply cut ties with parents who don't have their best interests at heart. Some have trusted the wrong man or walked down the wrong alley at night. It's sad, but it's just one of those things that happens.

Ro used to live in New York; she knows how dangerous the world can be. She carries pepper spray and doesn't visit dangerous places after dark and threads her keys between her fingers like Wolverine when she walks through the Target parking lot at dusk. Whether for better or worse, Milla Fairfax is probably long gone.

Ro locks her car doors before crumpling up the flyer and tossing it in her bag.

3

All week, Ro tries to focus on her work, but her mind often wanders back to the farmers' market, to the very specific full-body shiver she felt when she entered the booth and saw Ash again. It was like Christmas morning as a little kid, when her dad turned on the lights and she could finally see what had been waiting in the darkness, the wrapping paper shining and toys and candy peeking enticingly out of her stocking. She can't wait to feel that again.

But Ro has worked very hard to get where she is. Instead of spending her summers traveling, she spent them taking classes so she could level up faster. Instead of spending her weekends partying, she claimed her favorite carrel at the library and hid behind a stack of books. And yes, okay, so she preferred reading and researching to a loud room full of strangers, but the point is that she has put in the hours and made many sacrifices to be in her dream job this early in her career. Well, the first stages of her dream job. Tenure is still very far away, but she is barreling toward it with dogged persistence because that is what she does, and a peculiar curiosity about some random soapmonger isn't going to change that.

That's what she tells herself, at least.

Still, each time she puts down her pen and takes a forkful of cupcake, her eyes roll back in her head and she falls away into daydreams about French markets and fields of wildflowers and gazebos full of twinkling fairy lights, and in these daydreams there is a blonde girl smiling at her.

She wants to see Ash smile again.

It is very difficult neglecting the little plant. It doesn't change at all from day to day, but the soil looks dry. Ro sticks a finger down into the dirt, googles snake plants, and contemplates giving it just a little bitty sip, despite what Ash told her to do.

But then she knows Ash will ask her if she watered the plant, and she is not a good liar, not when it counts.

She does not water the plant.

She names him Tybalt because he is small and spiky.

She wonders if Ash names her plants, if she gets attached to some of them and can't sell them. She thinks about Tybalt sitting on a shelf in Ash's house, exchanging atoms of oxygen and carbon dioxide with her. She puts her face near the plant and breathes in deeply. She imagines she smells roses.

4

On Friday night, Ro is too excited to sleep. She wants
to see Ash again, discover what she's wearing, report
on her plant, which is not yet dead. She made the cupcakes
last as long as she could, which was exactly four days. Maybe
tomorrow she'll buy seven, a rainbow of pretty pastel colors to
line up in her fridge and savor all week. One of the marvelous
things about being an adult is that she can eat cake for breakfast
anytime she likes. She rents a little two-bedroom house with
a rickety porch and wonders what it would be like to be part
of a generation that could afford to own a house and take
extravagant vacations at her age, but is also somewhat charmed
by the feeling of freedom she gets from owning nothing, from
owing nothing. At least her scholarships got her through school
without student loans. At least she isn't in thrall to her mother.
At least her job pays fairly well and her book earned a nice little
bonus from a small press. She may not have married up, like her
mother raised her to do, but she is satisfied enough with what

she has. She is responsible for herself and her cat, Anon, and no one else.

Well, and Tybalt, the snake plant.

She watches *Pride & Prejudice* until she falls into an uneasy sleep and wakes tangled in her quilt. She drinks her coffee and watches the sun rise on the porch with Anon on his harness and leash so he can't wander too far. He just likes to roll around in the clover, really. When he jumps in her lap, there is pollen caught in his striped fur and he butts his head under her chin and purrs. She wonders if Ash likes cats. She seems catlike, perhaps – aloof and precise, sleek and pretty.

When the time is right, Ro gets dressed, this time in a fluttery white tank that feels carefree and her favorite jeans and sandals that show off her toes, which are painted the same butter yellow as the frosting on the cupcakes she's devoured. She listens to her favorite playlist on the way to the market, smiling with the windows down, every nerve tingling with anticipation. She forces herself to wait in the car until the market has been open ten minutes so she won't seem as desperate as her heart suggests she is. As she walks down the aisle of stalls, she feels like a raw nerve – the jute bag rubs the soft place under her arm, the sun pierces her eyes, the scent of sausage eddies along the asphalt like fog.

And then Ash is there, behind the table, as if waiting just for her.

Ash is smiling at her, showing her pointy little cat teeth. Her hair is in two loops and she's wearing a sundress, soft periwinkle, her white shoulders curving like bird wings.

"Still alive?" she asks.

Ro holds up her phone. "Yes, but then again, you ordered me not to kill it."

Ash comes out from around the table to take a closer look at the screen. Ro was careful to take the most aesthetic photo she could, one that showed her home to its best advantage. Tybalt sits just beside a sparkling clean window in a white ceramic pot she bought at Target because the grower's pot seemed almost like underwear, like something that wasn't meant to be seen. Beside the plant she's arranged a grouping of books between two marble bookends — her favorites from Shakespeare, naturally, plus a few prized editions of Austen and Brontë. And a copy of her own book, a decision she agonized over for far too long. It is an Instagram-worthy photo, an Ikea ad-worthy photo. It is a photo that says, *Go on, develop a crush.*

After inspecting the image, Ash smiles and nods approvingly. "Good. When you get home, go to the sink and hold it under the faucet until water runs out the bottom of the pot. Give it a few minutes to stop dripping, then put it back in the ceramic pot in that same exact spot by the window. And then don't water it for two weeks."

"Two weeks? Won't it die for real, though?"

A secretive smile. "Nope. Like I said: neglect it."

Ro slips her phone back in her pocket, slightly disappointed. If she isn't supposed to water Tybalt for two weeks, does that mean Ash doesn't expect to see her for two weeks? She will go absolutely mad in that time. She has barely exchanged a hundred words with this girl, and yet she feels like she will stop breathing without her.

"So that's how you treat all your plants at home?" she asks, clearly fishing.

"That's how I treat my snake plants. Other plants have other needs. I give them what will help them thrive. I have a little greenhouse and a potting shed out back. Make my own compost and fertilizer so I know exactly what they're getting."

Oh, how Ro longs to see this greenhouse, to see if it matches the lush, living picture in her head.

"Do any of your plants at home ever die?"

Ash shrugs. "Not often, but sometimes. No matter what you do, even if you give a plant everything it needs, some will fade."

"And then what?"

"And then it goes into the compost bin to feed other plants. You can't feel too terrible about it. Everything dies, and nothing has to go to waste. Speaking of which…" She goes to the table and holds up another cupcake, this one with frosting the light caramel brown of Anon's nose and the little brown flecks on his tummy. "This week's special. Maple bacon." But she doesn't hand it to Ro — oh no. She peels back the wrapper and holds it up to Ro's face, forcing her to take a bite or look like an absolute asshole.

Ro is very, very glad that she French-braided her hair. She takes the bite.

Good God, what magic Ash has! The salty fat of the bacon, the sweetness of the maple, the indelible creaminess of the frosting, the toothsome chew of the cake. It might be the best cupcake she's ever had. She realizes her eyes are closed and feels like an idiot. She stops rolling the bite around her mouth and swallows.

"Oh my God," she murmurs. "I've never tasted anything that good in my entire life. It's the apotheosis of baked goods."

Ash beams. "That's what I like to hear."

For a moment they stand there, the bitten cupcake between them. Ash seems curious, like she's waiting to see what Ro will do next. Ro, too, is waiting to see what she will do. Why does she feel like it's up to her, like she's stuck in the middle of a Choose Your Own Adventure book?

"Looks like I'm buying that one," she says. "But I'll definitely need to make it a four-pack."

The spell broken, Ash moves back behind her table and unfolds a box. "What other flavors?"

Ro's eyes rove over the candy-colored cupcakes. "You choose for me."

"Oh, I like that," Ash says, her voice going a shade deeper. She takes her time selecting from the dozens of cupcakes and chooses only the flavors Ro hasn't had yet.

When she picks up a strawberry, Ro flinches. "Maybe not fruit ones?"

Ash cocks her head. "But you liked the lemon."

"Lemon doesn't quite count, does it? Not like berries. I don't tend to like fruit that's been adulterated, outside of bananas and sometimes lemons."

Ash considers this, then places the strawberry cupcake right back into the box. "This will change your mind," she says.

"I'll come back next week and let you know." Ro is surprised by her own bravado.

Ash smiles impishly. "Good. I can't wait to hear your thoughts."

Relief descends as Ro realizes that Ash wants her to return — that maybe Ash keeps giving her reasons to come back on purpose. Whatever dance they're doing, Ash seems to know some of the steps. Or maybe they're both just stumbling around happily in the dark to the same tune.

Ro wants to stand here all day, but this is a business, after all. It would be silly to buy more soap. She doesn't need the weight of another plant. She has her cupcakes. There's nothing else to do here except make awkward small talk, and she's terrible at that.

"I guess I should pay now," she says, holding out her card.

"It'll be ten," Ash says. Still the friend rate, then. "Oh. Frosting." She reaches out and delicately dabs a bit of frosting off Ro's nose.

Ro is mortified and also mesmerized. Her nose tingles. "Thanks. Wouldn't want to go wandering around the market looking like a fool."

"You didn't look like a fool. You looked like someone who enjoys delicious things."

Ro takes her card back and nods. "That's apt enough. Thanks again."

"See you next week, Rosemary Dutton."

Ro gives a little wave and leaves with her box of cupcakes and the ghost of Ash's touch on the tip of her nose. It's odd, that Ash knows her full name and she knows only what she assumes is a shortened nickname of something that apparently isn't Ashley. There's an intimacy to a name, and the current imbalance makes things feel one-sided.

But! She used her card, which means her bank statement will have to list the business name, won't it? She checks the app once she's in the car. *Ash Apothecary LLC* is all it says. When she googles that, she finds nothing. No website, no Facebook page, no reviews.

The mystery remains.

She is not deterred in the least.

5

The week drags on. Ro teaches her classes, sits in her tiny office with the burgundy leather chairs and the desk so big and scarred it must be sixty years old. She thinks of it like a sleeping grizzly briefly in her care. She listens to her freshmen students sitting on the other side of that desk as they turn into whiny children when they can't sweet-talk her or threaten her into better grades. She marks papers at home on the porch, her mind wandering as she sips iced sun tea and eats delicate bites of Ash's cupcakes. She is torn between wanting to gobble them down at midnight like some dark ritual, and trying her best to make them last, to stretch out each morsel so that she can keep the richness of the frosting on her tongue.

Ash was right. This strawberry tastes different, somehow.

Ro has always hated fake strawberry flavor, resented that it was sour when it should be sweet, wet when it should be firm, syrupy when it should be tart. But Ash has somehow managed to capture a wildness, a freshness, a realness that she has never tasted before. Ro would have preferred to have two maple bacon cupcakes, but it's a curious experience, being over a quarter of a century into being alive and discovering that she doesn't hate something she was certain she hated.

She waters her snake plant like Ash told her, although it feels wrong to drench a plant like that when she's admitted to murder by overwatering. Ash was right again, though: the little plant continues to thrive, sitting proudly in her window. She thinks perhaps it needs a friend, now that her confidence is bolstered. If it is eventually going to die, it shouldn't die alone.

On Saturday morning, she stands before her closet feeling like she's thirteen again and unsure of who she is, much less what she should wear to broadcast that to the world. Ash has left her thoughts and feelings in utter disarray. She thought she knew who she was, but if she likes Ash the way she thinks she does, she might be someone else. She's accustomed to the sort of clothes that help her blend in and be taken seriously among other scholars: skinny jeans, sturdy boots, jackets and blazers — a kind of armor against the way men send out feelers to test a girl's vulnerability, a uniform that earns her students' respect and keeps her off the radar of her superiors. She's grown comfortable in dark colors, in somber, boring anonymity. But Ash makes her want to be soft and open, to feel the breeze on her bare legs and her hair dusting her collarbone. Ash makes her want to open like a flower.

Ash makes her want to wear pastels.

It's disconcerting.

And her wardrobe is not prepared.

She settles on a poet's blouse tucked into jeans, her gold sunshine necklace, flats that were made to look effortless even though they left her ankles bleeding for a week before they softened up. Her hair is in loose waves, her wrists jangling with bracelets. This is still her; a version of her. There are many, she tells herself; she can try them on as needed.

❦

The morning is blue and beautiful, and she sings at the top of her lungs, windows down and hair streaming. She almost gets pulled over by a sneaky cop hiding behind a neighborhood sign but manages to brake just in time; being happy always makes her drive too fast. As she walks from the parking lot to the market, a woman hurries toward her, eyes red and hair disheveled like she simply stopped caring.

"Have you seen my daughter?" she asks, holding up the same flyer Ro found under her windshield last week.

"No, I'm sorry," Ro says.

"She was here," the woman goes on as if caught in a panicked loop. "She told me she would bring me strawberries for my birthday, but I haven't heard from her."

"I'm sorry." Ro says again and steps back, worried the woman will grab her arm like the wart-nosed witch from some old fairy tale. "I hope you find her."

"Be careful," the woman says before turning to the family coming up the sidewalk. "Have you seen my daughter?"

Ro pities this woman. She knows plenty of people her own age who have gone no-contact with their families due to bad behavior and bigotry, and she wonders if the girl is really missing or just blocked her mom and moved on with life on her own terms. She once wondered how her own mother would react to being blocked and unfriended, and the answer was a long, self-righteous email about how Ro was a bad daughter. Her mom wouldn't even know if she disappeared, and she definitely wouldn't be handing out flyers. But then again, some mothers push and some mothers pull, and this mother seems like she might be the kind of desperate Charybdis that a daughter might need to escape.

On her way down the aisle of stalls, Ro stops to buy a bag of jerky, a green box with four perfect peaches, and a dainty ring with a moonstone that has no business being so cheap. It feels new on her pinky, something she hasn't tried before. It's nice, doing something unexpected; it makes her feel like anything is possible.

As she approaches Ash's booth, she slows. Ash is arranging the pots on her shelf, filling in spaces to show the little plants to their best advantage. She's wearing a long dress, dusty mauve with puff sleeves, and again those light brown boots, their tips dusted with dried mud. Ash's hair is in a loose braid that falls over one shoulder. She looks up sharply, frowning, like Artemis caught bathing in a glade. But on seeing Ro, she smiles.

"How long have you been standing there?" Ash asks.

"Not long." Ro hopes she sounds easy and not caught out.

Ash crosses her arms. "Are you here to tell me how much you hate strawberry?"

Ro's cheeks grow hot. "You know I'm not."

A nod of triumph. "That's what I thought. What can I get you this week? The special cupcake is red velvet."

"My favorite. Maybe two of those, plus a lavender and a vanilla."

"I don't get to choose this week?" It comes out playful, teasing, like they're deciding who will lead in their ongoing dance.

"Did I choose poorly?"

At that, Ash laughs. "I can't say you did." She goes to the table and picks up a sample of the red velvet, holding it out for Ro to eat from her hand. Ro takes it delicately, awkwardly, with no way not to brush her lips against those long, smooth fingers.

This is red velvet like Ro has never tasted before, rich and deep.

"I don't know how you do it," she says after savoring and swallowing. "They just keep getting better."

"That's the goal." Ash packages up the cupcakes Ro has requested.

"Maybe some honeycomb this week, too?" Ro asks. "I've been doing more cheese plates lately."

Ash puts a jar beside the cupcakes. "And how's your plant?"

"He's chugging along, just like you said he would."

"And you haven't been tempted to water him?"

Ro shakes her head. "Tempted, yes, but I resisted. I just gave him that drenching you suggested. I tend to yield to expertise." She looks down at the golden honey, runs a finger along the label on the jar: *Ash Apothecary*, in dusty sage with little sprays of flowers. "I was thinking he might need a friend, actually. Don't most things do best in pairs?"

Ash smiles knowingly. "That's what they say." She walks to the plant shelf and looks it up and down critically. "I only

41

brought the most basic snake plants, but I have some more unique cultivars back home. Moonshine and jade. Would you like to see my greenhouse?"

That jolt Ro feels is akin to when the roller coaster takes off down the first hill. "Sure. If you don't mind."

"Stop by this evening, if you're free. Around six, maybe?"

"Six is good," is what Ro says, but what she really means is, *I would cancel literally anything to be there.*

"Give me your phone."

Ro unlocks it and hands it over without a thought. Ash pokes around, and when she hands it back, the map app is open with a new destination. It's out in the country, farther out than Ro has been since she moved here, but — well, if someone is going to have a greenhouse, a garden, and an apiary, they're going to need space.

"I'll be there." She tucks the phone back in her pocket and pulls out her wallet. "What do I owe you?"

"Always in such a hurry," Ash muses.

Ro looks around sheepishly. "I don't want to interfere with your business. Or bother you."

"You don't bother me."

Ro feels her dimples come out. "Good to know." She holds out her card, and Ash runs it through her iPad. "Do you have a website or an Etsy shop?"

Ash's brows draw down in a little V: a brief moment of frustration. "No. I don't like all those layers. I only sell in person. And they carry my work in several shops downtown. The thought of something getting lost in the mail and some anonymous harpy leaving me a bad review that I can't fight is infuriating."

Ro nods. "I grok that. I'm a college professor, and I live and die at the whims of student surveys. Of course, the kids who won't do the most basic work shout the loudest that I'm the unfair one. Anonymity can be a curse. And the postal system, of course, is a whited sepulchre."

Ash's eyes twinkle as she holds out Ro's card. "You really have a way with words."

Ro wishes to thank her grandmother for giving her that giant dictionary when she was eight. "Thanks. Words are my world. I teach literature."

She doesn't have to say at which college. There is only one.

"But you're so young."

"I get that a lot. I'm an assistant professor. That's our entry level, hence me teaching summer classes. But I did graduate high school at sixteen and get my bachelor's in three years."

That little V forms again. "So are you one of those people who only value degrees and grades?"

"I — no. I'm not an elitist." Ro is, but she doesn't want it to be a turn-off. "What's that old saying about how, if you judge a fish by whether it can climb a tree, it'll spend its whole life believing it's stupid? I think there are myriad kinds of intelligence. My grandfather didn't go to college, but he could take apart a car engine and put it back together, and that's a lot more useful than deconstructing Hemingway. So is baking, and making soap and candles, and — everything you do. When the zombies come, you'll be the queen and I'll be fodder." Ro knows she's rambling, but she sensed a precipice there and wants to backtrack until she's too far away to fall from it.

"Oh, I wouldn't let the zombies get you," Ash muses. "Professor."

"Assistant Professor," Ro corrects as she blushes, because along with her love of words comes a need for specificity and exactitude.

Ash looks over Ro's shoulder to the market beyond. This tent feels so intimate, so quiet and calm, that Ro forgets there's a huge crowd out there. While they talk, people wander past, but for no reason she can name it's rarely busy when she's here. She knows Ash must sell a ton; Ro gets here relatively early, and already the cupcake stand has been decimated. She follows Ash's glance but doesn't see anything unusual beyond the tent.

"Look, this is a huge ask, and I hope it's not out of line," Ash starts, looking unsure and a bit embarrassed, "but would you mind watching my stall for a few minutes while I run to the restroom? There's not a line for the porta-potties right now."

Ah. That's what she was looking at — that row of green boxes stinking in the heat. Ro is somewhat stunned that Ash isn't some sort of ethereal elf above such earthly triflings.

"Sure. I wouldn't mind at all. Although I don't know how to ring things up..."

"You don't have to. I'll be quick. If anyone comes in, just tell them I'll be back in five." She grab's Ro's shoulder, squeezes it. "Thanks. You're a life saver."

Ash darts into the crowd and disappears into one of the green boxes, and Ro finds herself alone in the stall. She moves to stand behind the table so anyone stopping by won't think she's just some rando. She peeks under the table but sees only a reusable shopping bag full of packing supplies and a worn canvas tote. She is desperately curious about Ash and nudges the tote with her foot to see if it'll slouch open and reveal something, anything — a book, a keychain, a favorite lip balm.

But then the customers arrive.

A well-kept woman in her forties wearing a tennis skirt steps in to smell the soaps and promises she'll be back in ten minutes to make her purchase. An older man with a cane inspects a jar of honey and asks if she'll take five dollars instead of ten. A skulking tween boy makes a beeline for the cupcake samples, and she sternly tells him there's a one-per-person limit before he goes feral. He grabs two and runs. It's kind of fun, watching the stall, but she does feel helpless, since she can't do much more than tell people that the proprietor will return soon.

As she rearranges the samples so they won't look so lopsided, a girl steps up to the stall. She is maybe a few years younger than Ro, angular and thin, with curly hair and a posh hippie vibe that Ro admires but can't pull off. Ro is not the kind of person who will set foot out of the house braless, whereas this girl…

"Is Ash here?" she asks with a little bounce.

Ro's hackles invisibly rise, but she pastes on a bland smile. "She just stepped out. Should be back in five."

The girl pouts. "But I want cupcakes."

"You're free to try a sample, and by the time you pick what you want, I'm sure she'll be here."

The girl steps to the table and pushes a sample of the red velvet in her mouth with one finger, moaning orgasmically. "I swear, these things taste like sex," she says.

"Did you try the maple bacon last week?" Ro asks.

The girl's head jerks around. "Maple bacon? There was maple bacon?"

A warm smugness drives Ro's smile. "I bought two. They were incredible."

"I want to try maple bacon." The girl sighs and selects another sample, cramming it in her mouth.

"Did I miss anything?" Ash says as she slips behind the table and bumps Ro with her shoulder.

"One lady is coming back to buy some soap, an old man tried to swindle me, and a kid with a dirt mustache stole two samples despite my grim chastisement. And then there's — "

She looks at the girl with the cupcake crumbs on her chin.

"I'm Jessie," she says with a toss of her dark hair. "Ash knows me. I'm here, like, every Saturday." She leans forward over the cupcakes, showing skin down to her navel. "I heard there was maple bacon, and you didn't save me one?"

"They went quick." Ash's smile is as tight and polite as her voice. "What can I get you?"

"Um…a red velvet, a strawberry, a lemon, and…what do you think? What's the yummiest?" She sways as she looks up at Ash, lower lip poking out.

"They're all good." Ash folds up a box and puts in three cupcakes. Ro — still on the wrong side of the table because Jessie is taking up all the breathing room on the other side —

notices that Ash doesn't take the time to pick the biggest, prettiest cupcakes; she just grabs whatever is nearest. Two of them touch in the box, and she doesn't seem to care. Ash never lets her own cupcakes kiss. This little detail plucks at Ro's heart.

"Another red velvet, then. Like I told your helper..." Jessie throws her chin at Ro. "They taste like sex."

Ash drops the fourth cupcake into the box and closes it. "That'll be fifteen."

The girl hands over three fives in a tight little roll. Ro imagines it's warm from her body. "I want that maple bacon next week, Ash," she says with faux sternness.

"We'll see what happens."

"I'm going to enjoy these." Jessie takes the box and turns, swinging her hips as she leaves.

The tension breaks, and Ro moves back around to the right side of the table.

"Thanks for watching the booth. Sorry you had to deal with that," Ash says, entering the sale in her iPad. "She can be a bit much."

Ro doesn't want to say it, but she can't stop herself. "Does she come here often?"

Ash doesn't look up. "Every Saturday. Usually at opening or closing, when things are quiet and I'm a captive audience. I don't know anything about her, other than she's a theater student — not a particularly good one — and she really likes my cupcakes."

"Well, to be fair, they're truly excellent cupcakes."

Ash looks up with a smile. "Thanks."

Ro is trying to think of some logical reason to stay just a few moments longer when Ash looks past her and...changes. Her posture, her smile. She's bright but dulled. That smile is fake, but Ro wouldn't know that if she hadn't spent three weeks contemplating the real one.

"Hi! Can I help you?" Ash asks the admittedly attractive guy who has just entered the booth. He looks like he's thirty and sings with a punk band — built, tattooed, perfectly flopping hair, black shirt aged just enough.

"It's my mom's birthday tomorrow," he admits with a gleaming but slightly crooked smile. "Could you maybe put something together for me?"

Ash comes out from behind the table, puts a hand on Ro's forearm. "I'll see you tonight, right?"

Ro looks at the hand, looks at Ash's face, and pastes on a fake smile of her own. "Definitely. Thanks again."

"No, thank you. You saved me." Ash squeezes Ro's arm, releases her, and goes to the soap rack, picking up a bar of rose soap. "You might want to do a floral-themed gift," she tells the guy, her voice bright, "if your mom is into that?"

Ro recognizes that she has been dismissed, and she now feels like a third wheel. She picks up her box and honey and heads out. Ash is laughing with the guy as holds up soaps for him to smell, and it makes Ro feel hollow and strange. Which is the real Ash? Ro herself has many faces, many facets: the stern lecturer, the quietly dedicated student, the aggressive researcher, the excited theatregoer bouncing in her seat. Does Ash, too? Is this just what it takes to sell things at a farmers' market — pretending to be interested in everyone who stops by?

Yes. And yet...no. The face Ash shows her must be the real one. Ash touched her. Gave her real smiles. Called her a life saver. Reminded her to be there tonight. Ash can fake friendliness with some cute guy, she can fake tolerance with Jessie, but she can't fake an invite to her home.

And still Ro is jealous, and she knows she has no right to be.

Why is she living and dying by this strange girl she barely even knows? Why does Ash make her feel like Brian Welch did in eighth grade, when her entire day's mood was determined by whether he was in school or not, despite the fact that he didn't know she existed? Why does she wait all week just to stand here for ten minutes in a haze of confusion and hormones?

They have a connection — Ash has to feel it. Ro definitely does. It lives under her skin like an itch she can't quite scratch.

She goes home and eats honeycomb on crackers with another log of cheese from Belinda the goat and drinks her sweet tea on the porch with her cat twining around her ankles and deletes the dating app she put on her phone when she got the job and moved here after splitting with Erik. In her entire life, she hasn't spoken to a single guy who makes her feel like Ash does. Not even close.

She has a new job in a new town, is going to new places and trying new flavors. She might as well keep trying new things.

6

That evening, Ro contemplates changing into something different before going to Ash's house but is very aware that she doesn't want to look like she's trying too hard. Yes, she's just going to a merchant's house to look at plants, and yet it also kind of feels like…a date?

Why can't it be both? Why not both?

She brushes her teeth and hair, redraws her eyeliner, sprays on her favorite perfume. In the kitchen, she spends way too long deciding what to bring. She's southern, after all, and good southern girls don't go to someone's house without a gift, pie, or casserole in hand. She's narrowed it down to a bottle of Riesling or a hunk of brie she picked up at the French shop downtown. She easily axed the idea of flowers, as Ash is a gardener and that seems almost insulting. She's obviously not going to bake; she's decent, but Ash's cupcakes are exquisite. Cheese implies that Ash should have the rest of the fixings for a cheese board, and if Ash expects this visit to consist of a simple plant selection and exit, it will be impossibly awkward to hand her cheese.

So...wine is the smart choice.

You can invite someone in and open a bottle of wine, or you can thank them and put the wine up for later.

Yes. Wine it is.

Ro times it so that she arrives two minutes before six. Phones are wonderful for that, telling you exactly how long a journey will take. Ash lives maybe thirty minutes out into the country, where things are all spread out. The drive takes Ro past rolling hills and dilapidated barns and clusters of curious cows. She turns down a long driveway by a neatly kept mailbox surrounded by wildflowers, her car bumping over cracks and buckles in the asphalt. The fields behind the old wood fence on either side are fallow, their grass high and green. When the fields end, so does the asphalt. An old blue farm truck with a camper shell waits in a gravel circle like it was painted in to add extra charm.

Beside an ancient oak is a picturesque one-story farmhouse, exactly what she would expect of someone like Ash. Several outbuildings peek out from the greenery behind the house; Ro is pretty sure she recognizes a barn. The glowing green gardens around the front porch are clearly loved and well kept, with explosions of hydrangeas and the wafting scent of jasmine and honeysuckle. Hummingbird feeders, wind chimes, and suncatchers hang from the eaves. There's a porch swing, a rag rug, a pair of dirty old boots that must be too big for Ash's feet.

Oh.

Maybe she lives with someone.

Her mother, a roommate, a…friend.

Ro will find out soon enough. She gets out of the car and considers the wine bottle before stowing it in the floorboard. If Ash invites her in, she'll mention it; if not, she'll take it home to drink away her disappointment.

The front steps squeak under her flats as she steps onto the porch and knocks on the front door — there isn't a doorbell.

When the front door creaks open under her fist, she isn't sure what to do.

"Hello?" she calls. She peeks in, just a little, but can't see much, just white walls and warm wood tones. She knocks again, this time just to the side of the door. "Ash?"

She thinks about stepping inside, but…no.

She was invited here by a merchant to look at goods, not by an old friend for dinner. There's just something very personal about entering a stranger's house for the first time, and she doesn't want to do anything to jeopardize Ash's goodwill.

Instead, she heads around back, where the greenhouse would be.

There's an old path, worn gray stones with moss and dandelions growing between them. She passes between an enormous fig tree and a burst of butterfly bush and enters a veritable paradise.

Green is the predominant word that comes to mind. This place is so very green, so very verdant, so very lush, just a hair away from overgrown. The word bosky even floats up from some ancient vocabulary test, a word she rarely gets to use.

The tree branches hang low and the bushes crowd close on either side of the rambling path. At first, she thinks she sees an ancient umbrella skeleton, but then she realizes it's a clothes-drying rack. A chicken cackles in terror and darts away from her — a pretty black speckled hen with a jaunty red comb.

"Ash? It's me — Ro!"

Still no answer. She feels like she's in *The Secret Garden*.

She loves it.

She sees the barn now, a big old red thing with a barred door topped by a horseshoe. Rows and rows of raised beds hold a bounty of vegetables and berries. Bees buzz happily around sprays of flowering herbs, and she notices whimsical clay statues that ooze character — a charismatic tortoise, a cavorting hippo, a goddess-like woman with fragrant lavender bursting joyously from the crown of her head.

Aha!

The greenhouse comes into view looking like something Neil Gaiman built with his words. The base is hand-laid gray stone gone old and slick with age, but the top part is a mishmash of rippled stained-glass windows and dusty old panes that look like they were found on the side of the road. A shape moves within.

"Ash?" Ro calls.

Ash spins around, startled, and opens the greenhouse door, an old-fashioned screen one.

"You'll have to forgive me," she says with a bemused smile. "I lose all track of time when I'm in the garden." She has a flowered apron on over her mauve dress and a smudge of black earth on one cheek. Ro resists the urge to swipe it away.

"So this is where your plants come from?" she says instead.

"Some of them. Do you want to come in?"

Ash steps back and Ro enters. The greenhouse is the size of a small room and feels somehow both eternally sturdy and delicate as a soap bubble. It's a riot of plants, with various mismatched shelves and tables, every surface covered in growing things. One shelf is all orchids heavy with flowers. Another is covered in vines that twine around wire struts. There's a small lemon tree in a big clay pot, clustered with a lime tree and some small, orange citrus fruits — kumquat, perhaps? There are trays of seedlings and pots of flowers and one big cactus so tall she isn't sure why it doesn't fall over. But what she doesn't see are little snake plants.

"It's beautiful," she says, marveling at a spray of plum and pink orchid blossoms.

"Thank you. It's a labor of love."

"I didn't see these at the market." Ro makes as if to touch one of the blooms but stops just short of making contact.

"Orchids are picky." Ash subtly moves between Ro and the orchids. "I only sell plants your average shopper can keep alive. I don't want angry people bringing me dead plants every Saturday."

Ro winces and sidles away. "Yeah, that sounds like my version of hell. So are these the lemons that flavor the cupcakes?"

Ash reaches into the pocket of her apron and pulls out a wicked pair of silver shears. She snips a yellowing leaf off one of the orchids and tosses it in a compost bin before joining Ro by the lemon tree. She grasps the biggest of the lemons and gives it an experimental twist. To Ro's surprise, it pops off neatly in her hand.

"They are. And they're very good in sweet tea, if you like that."

Ro chuckles. "I'm from Savannah. I'm legally bound to like it."

Ash stashes the lemon in her apron pocket with the shears and cocks her head toward the door. "Want to pick out a snake plant?"

Ro takes the hint and exits. The greenhouse was a quiet, calm sanctum, but back outside she's met again with a riot of sensations: reaching branches and blowsy blooms full of butterflies and buzzing bees and a hundred perfumes battling for supremacy. Ash leads her around the path to a shed, what they call a "she shed" these days. Classical music dances on the breeze, so low Ro can barely hear it. The double doors are thrown open to show a space crowded with houseplants of all shapes and sizes. They hang from the ceilings, line the shelves, gently reach for her knees from pots lower down. Light strips illuminate everything, and there's an old Persian rug on the ground. A speaker tucked away somewhere gently plays an unaccompanied violin, something slow and sweet and seductive. Ro briefly has the thought that she could kill all of these plants in less than a week, but then she reminds herself that, with Ash's help, Tybalt is flourishing.

"So these are the ones you'll want to choose from." Ash indicates a shelf of plants that look like variations on Tybalt, some darker or more silvery or with brighter yellow stripes.

"Which one would you choose?"

Ash considers her. "Do you always let other people choose for you?"

Ro is slightly taken aback to be called out like this. She doesn't generally let other people choose for her, especially not in her studies or her career, where she's a fierce fighter and will butt heads with anyone who wishes to debate. But there's something about Ash that softens her, that makes her want to be more pliant.

"Only when I'm certain they know more than me," she admits. "I don't know the signs of a healthy plant as compared to one giving up the ghost. Now, if we were in a bookstore or a classroom, I would have definite thoughts."

Ash nods as if this is acceptable. "Look for signs of new growth. Avoid anything brown, yellow, shriveled, wilted, or crispy looking. Check the leaves for black or white dots or obvious bugs. And then just follow your intuition. Plants are living things, after all. They need sunlight and water, but they also need fertilizer and love. They like classical music, especially violins. Hence the Vivaldi." She steps back and holds out a hand in invitation.

Ro steps up and looks at the little plants arrayed on the shelf. There are a few dozen, at least, all jockeying for position like school children lining up for lunch. She splays a hand over them as if choosing a tarot card. Her fingers twitch, and she reaches for a silvery plant that just feels right.

"Moonshine. Good choice," Ash says, and something blooms in Ro's chest.

"I'll call this one Romeo," she says, holding it up and turning it this way and that, looking for pests as she was instructed. "So he can keep track of Tybalt."

"So they're both doomed?"

Ro feels a little lift as she turns to Ash. "Are you a fan of Shakespeare?"

"I remember beautiful things."

Their eyes lock, and the moment stretches out, the air heavy with summer's heat and the scent of deep, dark earth. Ro doesn't want to blink, doesn't want to breathe, doesn't want to break the spell.

"How about that tea?" Ash asks. "I baked some bread, too."

Internally, Ro shrieks, *But I didn't bring the cheese!*

Externally, she says, "I love bread."

Ash leads her back toward the house, and Ro feels an odd, timeless tug. It could be any year as she follows that swinging yellow braid and long dress among the overgrown shrubs and nodding flowers of the garden. They could be in an abbey's conservatory in the Middle Ages, in Van Gogh's asylum, in Elizabeth Bennet's backyard. At one point, Ash bends to snatch up a nut-brown chicken, muttering, "Honestly, Helen, you've got to stop doing this." She carries the chicken to a henhouse Ro didn't notice, off to the side of the farmhouse, and gently shoves the bird through a hatch set in the wire.

"She gets broody," Ash explains, "then hides her eggs from me. Almost like she knows where they end up."

She shuts the little door on the indignantly squawking hen and heads for the main house, untying her apron and hanging it on an ancient nail by the door. The covered back porch is less finished and formal than the front and seems mainly to be used for work things. There are tools hanging on the wall, garden clippers and limb loppers and shovels and trowels and a wooden broom. Everything has a pleasant sort of age to it, as if each item was purchased back when things were made well and then kept nice over the years by loving hands.

Ash holds the door open, and Ro steps inside. They're in the kitchen, which is bathed in early-evening light by a large window over the sink and another offering a garden view by the dinged wooden table. Everything in Ash's house is neat and clean, just so, an eclectic mix of old and new and everything in between. The mixer and the old mustard-yellow landline phone with its tangled curly cord have to be from the seventies, but the fridge is new and top of the line. The sausage grinder bolted to the table might be from the 1800s, and the sky-blue typewriter must hail from the middle of the previous century. Old farm implements and tasteful taxidermy mix with modern acrylic paintings of flowers. Ro is especially drawn to a square canvas of hydrangeas in a round glass vase and steps close to inspect it. She's always loved real paintings that show the artist's marks — glops of paint and dashes of bare canvas. The paint is thick, and some of it has cracked and fallen off a corner.

"I love this one," she says. "Where'd you get it?"

Ash glances over as she washes her hands at the sink. "I'm not sure. Some market somewhere, probably."

Uncertain what to do, Ro sits at the table with her plant. There's a curious intimacy to being in Ash's home. Ro's little house...well, it feels like a rental, like she moved all her things in but the house will go on in its own way when she's gone. It's a shell, and she's a hermit crab. But Ash's house has its own personality, like it has always been what it is and will continue to be this way. Ro can't imagine what it would look like if it was cleared out and dolled up to sell, the way real-estate agents stage everything with plain gray couches and glass tables. This house feels like it owns itself, like it's far from a shell that just anyone could inhabit.

She doesn't see anything to indicate a second person lives here, or even visits.

"How long have you lived here?" she asks.

Ash pokes around the fridge and pulls out a glass pitcher of tea. "All my life. My mom had me too young, and she didn't know who my dad was, so she left me with my grandmother and ran away. We never saw her again. My grandmother raised me. She grew up here, too. It's an old house." She fills glasses with ice and tea and brings them and a butter dish to the table. "Oh! The lemon."

Ro sips her tea while Ash runs out for the lemon, left behind in her apron pocket. She returns, cuts the lemon on the butcher-block counter, and drops a slice in each of their glasses, then brings over a round loaf of bread with a perfect X in the center, plus two silver butter knives and two white plates. Ro wonders if she should bring up the wine in her car, but Ash is setting the vibe, and she has chosen tea and bread. There's a wine rack on a shelf with at least six bottles in it, some red and some white, so either Ash drinks or she knows people who do. If Ash wanted to serve wine, she would.

Even before she bites into the thick slice of bread slathered in butter, Ro knows it's going to be good because she's beginning to suspect that Ash is good at everything. She does not expect the sparkles of salt in the butter, the perfect pillowiness of the bread. She does not expect to gobble the bread in a few bites and wonder if it would be rude to ask for more. Ash cuts another slice and places it gently on her plate, watching Ro spread the butter and take a bite, leaving perfect little tooth marks. Ro does not mind the way Ash watches her. It's not the way men watch her, as if for their own pleasure and amusement. Ash is studying her, maybe. There is a brightness to her eyes, a curiosity, like a bird. Ro likes it, likes to be seen this way. She thinks perhaps Ash likes to watch her enjoy things. This is not a terrible thought.

"Is the bread one of your grandmother's recipes, too?" she asks, halfway into her second slice.

Ash has only eaten a few bites; her bread sits forgotten on her plate. "It is. She taught me how to make it when I was young. It was our everyday bread recipe. She made sure I followed the directions perfectly, down to the ounce." That little V appears between her brows, and Ro longs to ask her what unfortunate memory has just surfaced, but she doesn't want to drive Ash away by psychoanalyzing her childhood during their first non-market visit. "I made the butter, too."

Ro looks down at the butter in the dish and notices it doesn't look like a commercially formed stick at all; rather, like it was pressed out of a mold. "How do you find the time?" she asks, incredulous.

Ash lifts a shoulder, which makes her dress slide deliciously off her other shoulder. Her skin is the color of cold milk and her bra strap is baby pink, and she quickly pulls her puffed sleeve back up. "This is my job, and I like this sort of work. Making things from nothing. Using the materials at hand so that nothing goes to waste."

"So this isn't a side hustle? This is all you do?"

Looking around the kitchen, Ash says, "When my grandmother died, I inherited the house and her savings. I live simply. The truck and my utilities are my only real expenses, outside of craft supplies. So I've never had to do anything else."

"That sounds magical." Ro hears the jealousy in her voice, and apparently so does Ash.

"But you like your job, don't you? Teaching?"

It's Ro's turn to shrug. "Not as much as I like other things. If someone would pay me to sit outside on the porch and read, that would be my ideal job. Until then, teaching isn't bad. A couple of hours a day, one afternoon of open office, some grading at home, and I'm done. At least it's not a nine-to-five sort of thing." She reaches for her glass and drains the last of the tea, enjoying the sparkles of sugar at the end — just like her own grandmother used to make it. As she sets the glass down, Ash reaches for it, and their fingers brush with an electric intensity, velvet throwing sparks.

"Sorry," Ro says.

"Thought you might need some more tea," Ash explains.

Then they both laugh, because they sound ridiculous. Ro pulls her hand away and Ash refills the tea, and then she drinks it and it tastes like summer in a glass.

Ro finishes her second slice of bread and Ash offers her a third, but she turns that down so she won't seem greedy, although she is. Ash doesn't finish her piece, but, well, this is her home and maybe she's already eaten. For Ro, the bread is a treat, a revelation; for Ash, it's the same old thing. Ash washes the plates by hand and sets them on a drying rack before refilling their glasses again.

"Want to sit on the porch?" she asks.

Ro nods. "I'd like that."

As she follows Ash through the living room, she notes the worn sofa with the afghan over the back, the old recliner, the bookshelf. What she doesn't see is a TV. In fact, she hasn't seen anything with a screen.

"Do you watch TV?" she asks as they step onto the front porch.

Ash sits on one side of the swing and Ro sits on the other. Ash rocks them with one foot on the ground, a comforting sort of rhythm. The shadows are going indigo, the last of the day's sunlight gleaming with desperation where it touches the glossy green leaves.

"No TV," Ash confirms. "No computer. No social media. No wifi. Just the landline and the iPad, but I only use that for work."

Ro's jaw drops without her consent. "Seriously? So it's just you and…nothing? Don't you feel unconnected?"

Ash kicks the swing back and forth. Ro lifts her feet and feels an easy, curious kinship, their bodies moving through space in tandem.

"You would have to be connected to later feel unconnected," Ash says. "I'm connected to this place and the land. What happens online isn't real, but this is real. Just look at it. Can a video of a cat falling off a table compare to that?"

Ro stares into the front yard, where bees buzz and butterflies dance as the swooping swallows get tangled up with newly woken bats. The air is full of soft sounds: the whisper of leaves and the sleepy clucking of chickens and the far-off bray of a donkey. She tries to think of anything better than this and she can't, except for maybe the ocean. Suddenly, social media seems absurdly silly. Ro loves words, but she loves real words, written words. Not hot takes and the terrible pun memes her mother delights in sending her because, even after twenty-seven years, she completely misunderstands her daughter. Ro loves Shakespeare and Pablo Neruda and Jane Austen. This garden — it feels like poetry, not a status update. It can't be captured in 280 characters.

"I take your point," she says softly. "It does feel terribly silly, compared to this. But ever since I finished school, it's been so hard to feel connected to anything. My plan was to get married to my boyfriend, for us both to get jobs in New York. But then he cheated on me and everything fell apart, and I realized all of our friends were his friends, and I'd been concentrating so hard on reaching my goals that I'd forgotten to be a person. I swore I'd never move down south again, but I needed something familiar, something… slower. I don't seem to fit in with my department here, though. I feel like a balloon bobbing about along the ground. Untethered. There's something in social media that provides a lifeline, even if it comes with a heaping helping of anhedonia."

Beside her, Ash chuckles, then softly bumps shoulders with her. "'A heaping helping of anhedonia.' That's just beautiful. Have you always had a way with words?"

"It started with Shel Silverstein and advanced at a troubling pace. My mom threw her back out for the first time helping me carry my haul of library books. I always preferred books to other children. People are difficult — they don't always tell the truth, much less know the truth — but books are honest." Ro doesn't want to stop having this conversation, doesn't want to stop swinging back and forth as their bodies lean ever closer, but... well, she's had three glasses of iced tea. "Can I use your restroom?"

Ash stops the swing, and Ro feels like she's out of rhythm with the world, which is not a new feeling.

"Down the hall, first door on the right," Ash says.

"Thanks."

Ro hops off the swing and goes inside, walking slowly to soak it all in. Everywhere she looks, there's something interesting she hasn't noticed before. She could spend an entire day with the bookshelf, which seems to have books spanning the past two hundred years. She reaches for an old leather-bound bible — but no. She's got a destination.

The hallway is painted cream with two doors on either side, all painted white with crystal doorknobs and all closed. She opens the first one on the right to a charming old-fashioned bathroom that must have been built or remodeled in the fifties, if the pink tile on the floor and shower wall is any indication. She handles her business, notes that at least Ash buys the good toilet paper, and resists the urge to open the medicine cabinet and see if there's evidence of anyone else in Ash's life. Before Erik, Ro trusted easily. Now, she's pretty sure she'll always be waiting for the other shoe to drop.

As she washes her hands, she recognizes the unique lather of Ash's homemade soap. The bar looks new, and Ro wonders if Ash put it out just for her. She doesn't recall gardenia among the market choices, but she knows this scent from her own grandmother's garden. There's a glass pump bottle of gardenia-scented lotion beside the soap dish, and as she rubs it between her palms Ro is certain that Ash made this, too. Even the fabric shower curtain looks hand-sewn. Everything she makes has a unique richness that is rare in today's world. The only art in this bathroom is a single painting by the same artist who painted the hydrangeas — a cheerful basket of geraniums, with a similarly chipped corner.

Before she returns to the porch, Ro peeks out the closed blinds and sees Ash still sitting in the same place on the swing, gently swaying. There's an attentiveness in the girl's posture, a sense of being awake and alert. Catching her unawares like this feels almost naughty.

Emboldened, Ro steps lightly back into the hallway and opens the next door on the right. It's a sunny bedroom done in pink with delicate flower patterns, simple but with elegant touches, including a big vase of mauve roses and a beautifully framed photograph of a ballerina in all white. She swiftly shuts the door and checks the one across the hall. This bedroom is bigger with its own bathroom and looks more lived in — it must be Ash's. The bed is perfectly made, everything exactly where it should be. Ro's mind gnaws on this fact; there are only so many reasons to clean one's bedroom to such a degree, the main one being that you expect someone else to see it. Perhaps Ash feels the same way Ro does — maybe she's even ahead of Ro when it comes to this thought process. Ro shuts the door gently and heads to the last door, the one across from the bathroom. She turns the doorknob and —

"What are you doing?" Ash asks.

She stands in the hallway like a ghost from another time, pale and...is she angry?

Well, she has every right to be.

"I was — "

Ash steps closer, stares at Ro's fingers on the doorknob.

"Don't."

Ro withdraws the hand, senses that she may have ruined everything.

"I'm sorry, I — "

"Curiosity killed the cat," Ash snaps. "If you're all done?" She stands closer to the door, forcing Ro to move around her to get out of the hall.

"You know, the actual quote is 'Curiosity killed the cat, but satisfaction brought it back,'" Ro says as she heads outside, cheeks hot with shame, hoping to salvage something of what was once a wonderful night.

"Probably helps if you have nine lives."

Ro holds open the door to the porch and Ash steps through it.

"I'm sorry — "

"Please stop apologizing. You're not ashamed of snooping, you're ashamed of getting caught. Snooping is rude. I expected better of you."

Ash doesn't sit back down on the swing, which means Ro can't sit either; she has to stand like a kid in the corner. She would like to dig a hole and die in it, but instead she's stuck on the porch feeling like a miscreant child. She has never been in this situation before.

"You're right," she says finally, a little breathless. "I suppose I expect better of myself. This…isn't like me." She looks into Ash's eyes, but she doesn't see hurt there — she sees fire. "Cards on the table: Ever since I caught my last boyfriend cheating on me, I've been paranoid. It broke me, and I never want to feel that way again. I have never been as curious about another human being as I am about you. I find you fascinating, and I like the way you make me feel. If you're seeing someone else, I need to know, now, before I get attached. I don't have a map for where I am or where I'm going. I'm floundering. So I suppose that constitutes my most pathetic excuse: I'm acting like a fool because you make me feel like a fool."

For a long moment Ash just stares at her, and internally Ro collapses like a blancmange. Perhaps she's been misreading signals. She has spent her entire life reading books about animals and people, and her life after puberty studying the words and actions and expressions of dead men, but she has never, before now, tried to decode a living woman to this degree. She waits for Ash to step back, to stutter, to make a joke, to ask her to leave, but Ash just considers her with an uncanny stillness, something swimming uneasily behind her eyes.

"It's unusual to meet someone who can put their truth into words, much less understand their truth to begin with," Ash says softly. "I supposed you've misstepped, but not tragically." She reaches out, puts a hand on Ro's forearm, bringing all the little hairs there to salute. "So I'll put my cards on the table, too: I'm a very private person. I don't invite many people here. I have boundaries. I need you to understand and honor that or we can't go on. This is a deal-breaker for me."

Hope sparks in Ro's heart. She might be forgiven, and they might go on. It's as if she's looking at the far horizon, seeing an island there after years adrift at sea, and she doesn't know what the island will hold, but she knows it might be home.

She nods. "I promise."

"I'm going to hold you to that." Ash's lips quirk, the tiniest smile, and then her other hand finds Ro's other forearm, and Ash leans in and Ro goes totally still, and there is a brief pause, a moment of searching question, and Ro feels her pupils widen like windows opening and her lips part just the faintest degree in welcome, and then she is being kissed, the lightest brush of warm lips, and her whole body fills up with rosy, melting heat, every nerve ending shooting off fireworks.

Ash pulls away and Ro is breathless, gazing at her in wonder.

"That felt like champagne," Ro says wonderingly. "Effervescent and ephemeral."

Ash's laugh bubbles up in a similar fashion. "You just don't stop. That's a bit delightful." She looks up at the darkening sky. "I have to do chores, but would you like to come over for dinner tomorrow, if you're not doing anything?"

Ro would burn her calendar for that chance.

"I'd like that. Can I bring anything?"

A teasing smile. "Maybe a bottle of wine."

Ro wants to say there's one in the car, that they can just keep on as they are, that they don't have to wait, that there are other dark places to explore. But she also recognizes that she has trespassed and been given a reprieve, and she will follow Ash's lead as they learn this new dance together.

"White or red?" she asks.

"Something with bubbles."

Ro nods. "I can make that happen."

"Oh! Don't forget your plant." Ash hurries inside and Ro stares out into the deepening shadows, feeling very much like an explorer in a new world who is finding nothing but wonders. As she gazes up at the stars, she appreciates the rarity of being so far away from the city lights that the sky looks like a great twinkling river. Ash brings out Ro's new snake plant plus the rest of the bread, tied up in a white cloth tea towel.

"I need to pay for the plant. And won't you need breakfast?" Ro asks.

Ash hands her the snake plant and tucks the bread under her arm. "The plant is a gift, and I can always make more bread. You enjoy it…and think of me."

Ro's grin could break her face in half. "That won't be a problem." Suddenly aware of her boldness, she hurries to her car. "Thanks for a lovely night!"

"Thanks for coming!" Ash calls back.

The whole way home, the bottle of Riesling rattles guiltily around the floorboard. Ro wishes she'd brought it inside… and yet she wouldn't change a thing about what happened.

Well, except for the snooping. She would definitely change that. She's ashamed at her brief loss of self-control there, and blaming it on Erik doesn't make that go away. At least she's learned her lesson early and well.

Ash is a very private person, and Ro promises herself she'll respect that.

Or try to.

She's just so goddamn curious.

7

On the way home, Ro gets a text from her department head, Dr. Drynen, a reminder that the theatre department is doing a fundraiser tonight and could really use butts in seats — her words, not Ro's. Drynen is a lifer, an old battleaxe, and Ro has been informed that it would be best to stay on her good side.

The show starts at eight, and Ro can just barely make it. Normally — well, post-Erik normal — Ro would ignore the email and stay home to enjoy the quiet, but being around Ash has emboldened her, made her feel like maybe getting out into the world isn't the worst thing. And not only that but there's a certain drama student she'd like to know more about.

Jessie.

The girl likely won't have a big part, considering Ash said she was terrible — but how does Ash even know she's terrible?

Ro has to go now, has to see if she can learn anything more. All she needs is a last name and the internet will reveal its secrets.

She hasn't been to campus much at night, but she finds a parking spot and walks toward the glowing lights of the theater. It looks so grand, with its soaring columns and classical pediment. Small groups stand outside, mostly students, talking and vaping. Ro wanders inside, glad that she already looked nice, as if she were merely a new professor coming here to support the school instead of veering off on a last-minute fact-finding mission after a quasi-date.

Luckily, she doesn't see anyone she knows on her way inside; she's focused right now and doesn't really want to make small talk. She pays for her ticket and finds a seat, wondering why she hasn't been here before. She loves theater, has been in the lights and backstage and running the front-of-house, and enjoyed every role. But since she moved here, it never occurred to her to even check into upcoming productions. Erik killed something inside her, but tonight Ash unknowingly started mouth-to-mouth, and Ro is finally waking back up.

Maybe Ash would like to come to a play, she thinks. A thrill runs through her as she imagines sitting here on the plush red chair, holding hands with Ash in the dark, sneaking glances as Ash focused on the stage, emotions playing over her face like wind in a field of flowers.

As she flips through her program, Ro holds in a silent groan. This isn't a play; it's a loose collection of monologues, scenes, and even some musical numbers. Which makes sense — the semester has just begun, so they won't have had time to prepare a full production. As her eyes skip to the names, she hunts for her prey and finds it — probably. Jessie Aleppo, doing a monologue from *Gone Girl*. That tracks. At least she's number six instead of number sixteen.

Ro settles in, resists the uncouth urge to poke at her phone. It's not that the theatre students are bad; it's just that her attention is elsewhere, in her heart and mind and dreams. When it's finally time for Jessie's monologue, Ro focuses on the stage, heart pounding. It doesn't occur to her until this moment that she's doing something...controversial.

It's not stalking, and it's not snooping, but it's definitely not innocent.

Does she think Ash is involved with Jessie right now and hiding it?

No. Ash seemed disgusted by Jessie.

But did Ash develop that disgust by dating Jessie in the past?

Maybe.

And when she laid it all on the line and told Ash that she needed to know if there was anyone else, Ash didn't confirm or deny. Ro was so grateful for her snooping reprieve that she skimmed right over that omission.

Jessie swaggers onstage in a striped shirt and skinny jeans and ankle boots, her hands in her back pockets. "Cool girl," she begins. "Men always use that as their defining compliment."

It's a little too on the nose for Ro's taste. Jessie isn't terrible — not *completely* terrible. She's exactly as terrible as any other college drama student who will never actually make it to New York or Hollywood. Listening to the monologue, watching Jessie go through her obviously rehearsed gesticulations, Ro doesn't learn anything new. But she has the girl's last name. She can look her up online now, even look her up in the system on her work laptop, although she isn't sure if that sort of thing is tracked. She has what she needs, and Ash will never know, and that's what matters.

She tries to sneak out at intermission, but Dr. Drynen spots her in the lobby.

"Love to see new professors involved in campus life," she says approvingly.

"Always glad to support our students," Ro responds.

She doesn't sneak out after that. She can't, not with hawk-eyed Drynen in the back row. Ro sits through every agonizing moment and is the first one to her car as soon as the curtain falls. She can't let Jessie see her. Can't risk Ash knowing she was here, even if work offers a perfectly good explanation. She feels only a little guilty. Ash may be very particular about her boundaries, but following her department head's orders is part of Ro's job.

When she gets home, the guilt evaporates. Ro goes into hardcore research mode. Unlike Ash, Jessie's internet footprint is deep and wide. Her Facebook isn't private, her Twitter is opinionated, her TikTok shows pretty much every inch of the apartment she shares with two other drama students. Jessie is... well, pretty much everything Ro doesn't like in another person: loud, pushy, overtly sexual in a way that feels disingenuous, free-spirited in a way that Ro will never be. There's even a video of her in a crop top eating one of Ash's cupcakes and making those same orgasm noises.

Ro doesn't learn anything she didn't already know. There is no mention of Ash, although scrolling back a few years on Instagram reveals boyfriends and girlfriends and Jessie's favorite way to open-mouth kiss whoever she's currently seeing while at a concert or party.

The most disturbing thing she learns is Jessie's age: twenty-one. That feels a little young, if she and Ash have been involved. But they probably haven't. Jessie isn't shy about spilling every detail of her life online, and the only evidence Ro can find that they even know each other is that one video of sensual cupcake destruction, and Jessie didn't even mention the source of the cupcake.

Ro closes her laptop, satisfied.

Mostly.

After Erik, she doesn't know if she'll ever feel safe trusting someone again.

But she's willing to try.

8

Sunday passes slow as molasses. All day, Ro eats Ash's bread: buttered toast for breakfast, an avocado BLT for lunch, cinnamon toast for a snack. It feels like a kind of transubstantiation. If the plants breathe out atoms that were once inside of Ash, the bread has been touched by her hands, her breath, the very cells of her body adding to the rise. It's not quite the same with Ro's basic store-bought butter, but she tells herself she will buy a butter dish and leave it out on the table to go soft, as Ash does. She likes the elegant simplicity Ash lives by, this philosophy of doing and making while wasting nothing.

As afternoon falls, Ro realizes that Ash only said "for dinner" without naming a real time, and they didn't exchange numbers. There is no way to get in touch with Ash, other than showing up at her house. Panic flares until Ro decides that if it was six yesterday, then six is reasonable for today. She puts on her favorite jeans, a flowy top, sandals, and layered necklaces.

It's odd, how hard it is to figure out what to wear on what seems like her first real date with another girl. When she's gone on early dates with guys, she was one side of the binary. The guy had masculinity covered, so she could project whatever kind of femininity seemed right for the occasion, whether that was glam, sweet, sporty, or whatever she thought would appeal to that particular man. But when there are two girls, she feels like she's sharing the entire realm of womanhood and doesn't want the pendulum to swing too far toward Ash or away from her. Ro would feel odd wearing a pastel cotton sundress and brown boots, but she would also feel odd in leggings and a leather jacket. So she just wears what makes her feel comfortable and pretty without trying too hard, because she is fairly certain Ash doesn't like things that are tawdry or overdone. Her reaction to Jessie at the market was immediate and telling.

As she drives, she sings along with Ricky Montgomery and lets the scent of the fields roll in through her open windows. In the passenger seat are a bottle of Prosecco and a small glass yogurt jar containing an interesting snail she found in her mailbox, along with a stick, some leaves, and a rock to make him comfortable. Again, she considered bringing flowers or candy or some other offering, but in the end she thought Ash might be most charmed by a simple snail with a shell the color of candlelit beeswax.

She feels it as she turns down the long drive — a lift in her chest, a tuning fork struck to produce just the right tone. Her car door closing is the loudest thing for miles. She carries the wine in one hand, the snail's jar in the other. A small table on the porch holds a charcuterie board, the strawberries still sparkling with beads of water and the cheese not yet sweating.

Ash knew she'd be here at six.

They already understand each other perfectly.

She knocks on the door, and this time Ash is quick to answer. She's wearing a white eyelet dress and her hair is pulled back with wisps framing her face. Her smile is shy and hopeful. She's been waiting for this, too.

"You didn't say what time," Ro starts, handing Ash the bottle of wine.

"I know. But you figured it out."

"Do you want to exchange numbers so it won't happen again?"

Ash rattles off her number, and Ro plugs it into her phone and calls so Ash will have her own number. The landline in the kitchen starts ringing instead.

"You don't have a cell?" Ro asks, confused.

"Don't need one. I have the iPad and go to a coffee shop if I need the internet."

"So I guess I won't be texting you, then." Ro is reeling. Outside of her ninety-three-year-old uncle, she doesn't know anyone who doesn't have a cell phone. And yet Ash has an iPad, so it's not like she's completely analog. It strikes Ro as odd, how selectively Ash uses technology.

Oh, well. At least she has the landline number now.

"It has an answering machine," Ash says, as if in apology.

"Cutting-edge technology indeed." Ro puts her phone away and realizes she has a snail in a jar in her armpit. "Oh, I brought you something." She holds out the jar, with its leaves and rocks and twig and curious snail, suddenly feeling even more awkward than usual. "I thought he was interesting."

"Most snails are hermaphrodites." Ash takes the jar and looks in at its tiny resident. "A glass snail, I think. Very cute. Pretty shell. Thank you."

Ash does look charmed, and Ro is glad she took the chance, even if it's weird. Why hide weird, she has always assumed, since it's going to come out sooner or later? Then again, she's talking to a girl who dresses like Laura Ingalls Wilder and doesn't have a cell phone, so there will be no Weirdo Olympics here. Ash has already taken gold.

"Can I fix you a drink?" Ash asks. "I make my own simple syrups, and they go well with Prosecco."

Ro could swoon. "That sounds amazing. Please."

Ash gestures to the charcuterie board. "Help yourself. I made the sausage and prosciutto and grew the strawberries, and the cheese is from a farm down the street. And the bread is mine, of course." Then, more shyly: "Hope you like it."

She disappears inside with the snail and Prosecco, and Ro hears the subtle pop as the bottle opens. The charcuterie board is so beautiful she almost hates to destroy it, but then she tastes the prosciutto and worries she will eat the entire board and be found gnawing the wood by the time Ash returns. Everything is delicious: the berries sweet and fresh, the cheese creamy and cool, the meats perfectly salted and — that word again — unctuous. The bread is cut and baked into buttery crisps, and even though she's eaten almost nothing but Ash's bread all day, she devours it.

Ash takes longer than Ro would expect, chopping something and rattling ice in a cocktail shaker before returning with two coupes made of thick, old-fashioned glass. Ro doesn't ask what she's being served, but the first sip assures her that Ash knows as much about cocktails as she does about cupcakes.

"Lavender and honey?" Ro asks.

Ash's face lights up. "Exactly. Do you like it?"

"I adore it."

"Oh! I forgot the tapenade." Ash runs back inside and returns with a ramekin. "You have to try it."

"I've never really been big on olives..." Ro starts.

"You said the same thing about strawberry cupcakes," Ash reminds her teasingly.

Ro tilts her head. "Checkmate. As you wish." She uses the bread to scoop up a bit of tapenade and chews carefully. It's briny, salty, astringent, sharp, the texture rubbery in the worst possible way. She forces herself to swallow it instead of spitting it out on the porch. She hates tapenade, but this one, unfortunately, seems especially horrid. "I'm sure you make the best tapenade in the world, but it's just not for me. It's amazing how such disgusting little fruits can make such delicious oil."

"Ah, well. I'm honored you tried it, at least."

For a few moments, they sip their cocktails and eat without really chatting, and Ro begins to wonder: How do you converse with someone who doesn't watch TV or movies or play video games? How do you relate? Does Ash read modern books? They haven't discussed anything of the moment, the sort of small talk that usually allows two people to recognize their compatibility quickly by discussing their favorite Marvel superhero or whether they think the Kardashians are interesting or abominable. She wants to ask a question but can't imagine where to begin. She considers several different avenues, and…

"Do you have a favorite chicken?" is what comes out.

At first Ash looks startled, then amused. "Yes and no. I try not to get too attached because I know how the life cycle works. There are raccoons and coyotes and hawks, and too many chicken diseases to list, and eventually they all stop laying and end up in the stew pot. When I was eight, my favorite chicken was called Amy after my favorite character from *Little Women*."

Ro locks that answer away as a big revelation of character.

"I raised her from a chick and pulled her around in my wagon and tried to swing her on the swing. But my grandmother discovered I'd snuck her into my bed and said I was getting too attached. That was the first chicken I had to kill, pluck, butcher, and get on the table all by myself." A sigh. "Chicken and dumplings. My choice. I wanted to do her honor."

"That sounds like the kind of short story they make you read in high school," Ro says, the bubbles already going to her head. "Ghastly but beautiful. Are you — I mean, did you like your grandmother?"

Ash looks off into the garden and sighs again. "When something is always there, it's beyond liking or disliking. She was all I knew. I respected her. She taught me everything. It was a cruel lesson, but…well, she was right. If you get attached to a chicken, it's still going to die, sooner or later. It's a waste, not eating it, even if it was your favorite."

"Well, sure, but it could die of old age while being pulled around in a wagon. I want to go back in time and give little Ash a hug." Ro tips back the last of her cocktail.

"She would've liked that," Ash says softly. "Let me refill that. The same, or something different?"

"Whatever you suggest."

Ash nods, takes the glass, and disappears. Ro hears the sounds of food preparation within, the clink of metal on ceramic, the hiss of steam, the soft thump of an old oven door closing. She smells meat cooking and immediately recognizes the scent of pork loin. Ash hurries out, hands her a full coupe, and heads back in, calling, "Dinner should be ready in a moment."

Ro hears sizzling inside, and her mouth waters as she wonders what's frying. She sips her drink and tastes roses and smoked rosemary. She's headed into tipsy territory, and she wants to wander drunkenly through the garden with Ash and ask her questions about every plant and every memory. Unless they're all like the chicken story. Ash's grandmother sounds like a piece of work, like she's from the 1930s instead of the 1990s. To make an eight-year-old kill and eat her pet? Horrifying. And that was, what? 2004? It sounds like something from the Depression.

Ro nibbles at the charcuterie board but is wary of eating too much, knowing that dinner is on the way. She doesn't want to get too full; she doesn't know how the night will go, but she has nebulous hopes she can't quite examine yet. She definitely wants to get the taste of the tapenade out of her mouth.

"Come on in and wash your hands," Ash calls.

Ro pushes open the screen door, places her coupe on the kitchen table, and heads for the powder room with barely a glance at the forbidden door. She is desperately curious about what's in there, considering there's not enough space for another bedroom and the house wouldn't need two bathrooms across the hall from each other. It would make the most sense if it was a closet, but Ash wouldn't be that protective of a closet. Would she? A memory filters down: Erik putting a password on his phone and laptop when they'd previously been unlocked. It didn't strike her as suspicious at the time, but now she's constantly looking for proof that something is amiss. Ro shakes her head and goes into the bathroom to wash her hands with the gardenia soap, dry them on the fluffy white towel, and luxuriate in the smoothest lotion she's ever touched.

When she returns to the kitchen table, she finds a beautiful spread of the kind of Southern food she remembers from her youth: pork loin with potatoes and carrots, black-eyed peas with rosy chunks of ham hock, sunny yellow creamed corn, floppy green beans, fried chicken livers, and biscuits.

"A smorgasbord," she intones, practically a prayer.

"I don't often cook like this, since my grandmother passed," Ash says. "It's nice to have a reason." She gestures to the chair at the foot of the table, and Ro sits down.

As Ash fills her plate for her, Ro asks, "When was the last time you had a reason?"

What she's really angling for is any evidence of Ash's dating history — is she into just women, or men and women, or is she, like Ro, trying something unexpected for the first time?

"My grandmother's funeral," Ash says, her voice low and flat, and Ro winces and realizes that she's made a mistake.

"It smells amazing."

She takes fork and knife in both hands and cuts her pork, but Ash says, gently but firmly, "In this house, we wait until everyone has been served and the blessing has been said."

Another strike. Two strikes, really.

Ro is botching this up terribly.

"Sorry," she mumbles. "I've been in college so long, I've become uncivilized. My Granny Carole would be rolling in her grave. And threatening to hit me with her cane."

Ash finishes serving herself and sits down. She folds her hands on the table and closes her eyes. After a significantly chastening look, Ro does the same.

"For this, and all we are about to receive, make us truly grateful. Amen."

"Amen," Ro echoes, finding it an odd sort of blessing. It didn't mention God or Jesus or love at all. She begins to think she would not have liked Ash's grandmother.

She opens her eyes and waits until Ash has taken her first bite before doing the same. As she makes her way around the plate, she's recalled to Christmas when she was tiny and the family would get together, every aunt vying to be the first with an empty casserole dish. Ash's cooking is both very traditional and yet elegant, the flavors balanced and the textures immaculate.

"The fried chicken livers are mind-blowing," Ro says between bites. "Everything is incredible, but I haven't had livers in years. They're so perfectly crispy."

Ash smiles. "I thought you might like them. Happy chickens make happy livers."

Ro looks at her plate, at Ash's plate, at the platter still half-full of little fried balls of meat. How many chickens did Ash kill? Or maybe she freezes all the chicken parts and defrosts them as needed? Maybe she buys them from a local farmer? It would take the entire henhouse to fill half that oblong platter.

Ro is not going to ask. The last time she asked about Ash's chickens, she didn't like the answer. Probably better not to know.

As she chews, she watches Ash between bites. Ash keeps all the food on her plate separated, taking delicate bites to mix the food on her fork. She didn't pile her own plate high, as she did Ro's, but she seems to be enjoying what she has. There's a daintiness there, a precision that Ro now connects to Ash's success as a baker and a maker.

"Do you like to cook?" Ro asks.

"When there's someone around to enjoy it. I can live off cheese plates and fruit and bread on my own. But make sure you leave room for dessert." After a few bites, Ash asks, "So do you have a lot of family?"

"My dad is dead and my mom is still in Savannah. She always wanted to retire out to Tybee, but the money just isn't there, which is apparently my fault. She likes terrible Facebook memes and stupid puns and watches too much Fox News. We don't have a lot in common these days, so I'm pretty low-contact. I'm an only child. When I was young and my grandmother was alive, we had big family gatherings with this kind of spread, but once we lost my dad and Granny, that sort of fell off. All the old people got old and all the young people moved away."

Ash asks her about her hometown, what she was like as a kid. Now, three drinks in and food drunk on top of that, Ro answers her questions and tells little stories and begins to notice that, when she asks Ash the same questions, Ash somehow turns them back around so that Ro is always the one who's talking. From what she can tell, Ash has never had much family — just her and her grandmother.

"It seems like you're asking all the questions and I'm monologuing," Ro says as she scrapes up the last of her creamed corn.

"I'm curious about you." Ash gives a shy smile. "And there's just not that much to my life. What you see is what you get. This place, and me."

"I'm fairly certain you have unplumbed depths," Ro teases.

Ash blinks up at her. "Oh, we all have our hidden places. But getting there takes time."

"I have a lot of time," Ro tells her, their eyes connecting with a jolt.

"I have all the time in the world." Ash bites her lip, a move Ro has never witnessed in real life, only read about in YA novels, but the effect is charming and vulnerable and beautiful and makes Ro want to cross the kitchen in three steps and kiss her.

She does not. She's fairly certain her teeth are full of corn.

"Ready for dessert?" Ash asks.

"I don't know where I'm going to put it, but I can't wait."

Ash goes to the fridge and pulls out a pie. Ro steels herself for it to be something fruit-filled and sighs in heavenly relief when she sees that it's a chocolate pie. Ash cuts a big slice and adds several strawberries to Ro's plate. She cuts a smaller slice for herself and takes her seat.

"I love chocolate pie," Ro says, digging in. "Oh my God, this crust is amazing! And the strawberries — the sweetest ones I've ever had, I swear."

Ash's cheeks pinken with pleasure. "Thanks. I've been refining my grandmother's pie recipe for years. Trying to get everything just right. Her crust was never fluffy enough."

"What's the secret?"

Ash chuckles. "Again, it's lard. Highly superior to shortening in every way."

Ro makes a vaguely orgasmic noise. "And the whipped cream. Hand done, I take it? I know that's not Cool Whip."

"Homemade is best. Cool Whip just tastes like chemicals to me."

Cool Whip doesn't taste like chemicals to Ro — she could eat an entire tub at one sitting without complaining — but she enjoys the thick, rich, creamy sensation of real whipped cream, just as she enjoys Ash's frosting. How the girl stays so thin and waiflike is beyond her. Ro has always worried about her weight, is always either on a diet or failing one or researching the next one, and she's a little worried that she's not as beautiful, as perfect as Ash. Then again, the way Ash is watching her savor her pie is...almost lascivious.

Maybe Ash likes her this way.

Maybe Ash likes lush curves.

The probing, eager, almost possessive look in Ash's eyes — it's emboldening.

What must it feel like, to be exactly what someone else craves?

Ro drags a strawberry through the whipped cream, pops it in her mouth, and bites down, dropping the stem on her plate.

"I've heard strawberries can be fickle," she says when she's swallowed. "Hard to grow, I mean."

Ash puts her chin in her hand. "It's like anything — if you know what they need and take proper care of them, they'll thrive. So not necessarily fickle, but they demand precision and maintenance. Most good things do." She pops a strawberry in her mouth, bites off the top with a juicy snap, her lips gone pink. "I don't think it's the worst thing, knowing what you need and waiting for it instead of settling for neglect or subpar attention."

Ro thinks of Jessie's obviousness and obliviousness. "I can see that. Specific cultivars require specific care."

"Some cultivars are rarer than others," Ash muses.

"What a gift, to discover such a one."

Ash throws back her head with a laugh like birdsong. "Such a way with words," she murmurs. "Want to sit on the porch? That's what I do instead of TV."

Ro stands, a little dizzy. She's had three drinks and Prosecco always hits her hard. "Sure. Can I help you clear the dishes first?"

"Absolutely not. I'll take care of them later."

"Then I'll meet you there shortly."

Ro heads for the restroom, and when she's done, she hurries past the forbidden door and finds Ash already on the porch swing, holding two glasses of white wine. Ash stills the swing and Ro sits, accepting the wine and sipping it. It's sweet, and she'll have to pace herself. She could drink a whole bottle of the stuff without really meaning to.

They rock and sip companionably, and Ro is painfully aware of the warmth of Ash's body, right there, so close, their elbows almost touching. She could easily hold Ash's hand, lay gentle fingers on the smooth curve of her eyelet-wrapped thigh. She has never touched a woman like that, has never wanted to before, but now she suffers the hopeful desperation of a child standing at the window of an ice-cream shop, aching to see the flavors and smell the vanilla sweetness of cones riding the air-conditioned breeze…but unable to open the door.

"You know — " she starts, but something rustles in the bushes, and she startles and focuses on the sound. "What's that?"

Ash doesn't appear concerned in the least. She didn't even jump at the noise. "Probably a chicken. It's Helen hiding her eggs again, I bet."

Ro is tense as the bush rattles again. It doesn't seem like a chicken. She doesn't know what she's worried about, just that her body is telling her something is wrong. It's dusk, and she can't see anything in the shifting shadows.

Much to her surprise, a raccoon waddles out, its face glistening as it licks its lips.

"That bastard," Ash hisses, going rigid. "He's been eating my eggs."

"Is that...normal?"

"They carry rabies and destroy plants and dig through the compost and steal eggs. A pestilence."

Ash silently stands and enters the house, careful not to make any loud noises. The raccoon snuffles along the ground as if it hasn't noticed Ro yet and is still hungry. It stops and sits up on its hind legs, using its adorable black-gloved paws to clean the egg off its face. Ro has never seen a raccoon up close like this. It looks young and sweet, and she is delighted to catch it unawares.

With no sound to herald her arrival, Ash materializes on the porch holding the shovel from around back. Ro's shoulders begin to rise up to her ears as she realizes what's happening. She's about to ask Ash what she's doing, why she's doing it, if she really has to — but Ash charges the raccoon, the shovel raised high overhead. It arcs down through the darkness and strikes the raccoon with a sickening thump. The raccoon gives a whimpering cry, and then Ro is frozen in horror as Ash beats it to death. Brutally. Ro can only stare, jaw dropped. The wine glass falls from her fingers and breaks on the old wooden boards. Her fingers creep over her eyes like she's watching a scary movie against her will. There is nothing she can say, nothing she can do. It is swift and savage and then it is done.

Ash stands and leans against the shovel, breathing heavily, her back to Ro. For a slight girl, Ro can now see that Ash has a wiry strength to her, the muscles in cords on her forearms. With a heavy sigh, Ash scoops up what's left of the raccoon with the shovel and carries it around back. Ro stares at the spot where it lay, its blood black in the dying light. Her gorge starts to rise.

Through the screen door, she hears the back door open and close, the kitchen faucet running for longer than usual. When Ash reappears, she smells of gardenias and brings Ro a new glass of wine, plus the bottle to top off her own glass. She uses her boot to scrape the broken glass against the house, away from Ro's feet.

"I'm sorry you had to see that," Ash says softly, sitting back on the swing and taking up her familiar rocking cadence. "It's one of the first lessons my grandmother taught me. If something threatens the farm, get rid of it. She welcomed snakes and possums, but she'd shoot a raccoon, rat, or coyote on sight. They get a taste for easy food, and they never leave."

"I understand," Ro says, although she doesn't. She sips her wine and clears her throat. "It's a shame they're so cute, though."

"Cute doesn't matter when it comes to threats," Ash says darkly. "I lost a chicken last week, and I bet he's the one who killed her. And my dog Pilot was bitten by a raccoon last year and had to be put down for rabies. It was awful. I was afraid it would hurt you. Just because they look cute doesn't mean they're not dangerous." Her hand slides over, her fingers twining with Ro's. "I can't stand the thought of it hurting you."

Ro exhales, her body relaxing at the touch. "It didn't seem like it was going to hurt anything…"

"It hadn't noticed us yet. That's why I had to hurry. Rabies — the early stages aren't obvious. They don't always foam at the mouth. I'm so sorry I scared you, Rosemary." She lifts Ro's hand to her lips, kisses it gently, a soft, warm touch in a big, dark world.

Rattled as she is, it does not escape Ro that Ash's dog's name is from Jane Eyre.

"I don't know much about rabies," she admits. "And I didn't know they kill chickens. I can see how that would be a problem for you. I'm just not used to...actually seeing violence, I suppose."

"When you grow up on a farm, it's a part of everyday life. It's the only way to survive."

This is...not how dates should go.

And yet, if Ash were a man, would Ro find this manly? Would it be more acceptable?

She isn't so sure. She's shaken. Possibly in shock. Ash's hand squeezes hers, reassuring her, tethering her.

Ro has family back in Swainsboro who hunt, who have deer mounted on their walls and big freezers full of feral pig meat. Her aunt married a hunter, and when Ro was young and they hosted Thanksgiving dinner at their farm, their boys would run around with BB guns, arguing over who'd popped the most rats in the barn. Her uncle shot coyotes whenever he could because, like this raccoon, they killed chickens, plus the barn cats. She watched it happen from their window once, watched the wild little dog-thing buck in the air and fall with a gasp after he shot it with his hunting rifle. She used to love the venison sausage for breakfast, the flavor of a turkey that had never been frozen. When she was ten, her cousin's neighbor gave her a squirrel tail like a knight presenting his lady with a trophy and she kept it in the back of her sock drawer for years.

Is this so different?

Would the stern pop of a gunshot be preferable? Is it the brutality of the shovel that's making it so hard for her to accept?

Sure, to Ro, the raccoon looked cute and sweet, but this is not her little rental house near downtown. This is a farm deep in the country, and Ash's livelihood depends on her ability to collect eggs, build compost, grow strawberries, and…well, not die of rabies. If Ro is going to get involved with a farmer, she's going to have to learn to live with farm life. Farmers eat the chickens they raise, and they have to protect the flock. Pa Ingalls would have done the same, she tells herself.

Ash drags Ro's hand into her lap, lets it rest atop her thigh. There are tiny red dots peppering the white fabric. "But enough about that. Let's talk of happier things. Tell me what you're looking forward to this week."

"Seeing you again," Ro says, shocked to hear it come out of her mouth. She definitely didn't mean to say that part out loud. She looks down at her wine glass and finds it almost empty. Her insides are as loose as good scrambled eggs, warm and golden.

"Well, that's easy enough to accomplish. I'm glad. After the raccoon, I thought…" Ash gulps down her wine. "I didn't know how you would take that. I was crying while I washed my hands."

She pours more wine for them both, and Ro doesn't think she needs any more but is already sipping. She's had enough now that it doesn't matter. She can't drive, and…well, she doesn't mind having to stay overnight, whatever that entails. She wants to know Ash better, to learn every inch of her, to be part of her life and not shy away when things get real. The raccoon was a shock, but Ro does not want to be seen as a prudish city girl, as someone too weak to deserve Ash's regard. Ash is strong and resilient and brave, out here on her own. She isn't lazy like Erik, who farmed his data entry out to his TAs. Ash does the hard work with her own two hands.

And still she cried at the sink. She feels things, deeply, just like Ro.

"No need to cry." Ro turns to Ash, cupping her jaw and rubbing a thumb over her cheek. It's not wet, but of course Ash would wipe her tears away before coming back out. "You have to do what you have to do."

Perhaps there is nothing to wipe away, but Ro doesn't let go, her fingertips light on Ash's jawbone. Ro is infinitely aware of the intricacies of the face before her, a face she's spent weeks trying not to think about constantly. She's beginning to feel swimmy and her eyes want to cross. She's so sleepy, but she wants to hold onto this moment forever.

"It's nice to be seen," Ash says, eyelashes sweeping down shyly. "I tend to feel rather misunderstood."

"The older I get, the more I feel like a singular species," Ro agrees, struggling to keep her focus but also finding an unusual fluidity in her words, like everything in her is becoming unmoored and nothing really matters. She leans forward, sets her forehead against Ash's, and slides her hand around to cup the back of her silky head. "Media told me I would have things figured out by now. That I'd know who I am and what I want."

"And what do you want, Rosemary?" Ash's voice is dusky as a dog rose.

"A myriad of things," Ro mumbles. "To be less drunk, for one. Here I am, right where I want to be, and I'm a complete idiot. Half asleep. Saying things I shouldn't. My filter has flittered away on the wind."

Ash pulls away and stands, leaving Ro to nearly topple forward out of the swing. The wine glass falls from her hand, and she loses track of it. She can only assume it shattered and made another mess, but she is having trouble finding the floor just now.

"Let's get you to bed," Ash says.

"No, not now. Not like this." Ro lets Ash pull her to her feet, and she feels like a brachiosaurus, big and unwieldy, her legs too far away to listen.

"You can stay in the guest room. It was my room when my grandmother was still alive. Come on, then."

The world passes in flashes as Ash leads Ro through the door, past the living room, down the hall, and into the smaller bedroom. The scent of roses washes over her as Ash pulls back the quilt on the bed, and Ro is embarrassingly aware that if she hadn't drunk quite so much, this might be a very different experience involving a bedroom.

"I didn't think I had that much wine," she says softly.

"All those bubbles," Ash says teasingly. "Let's get these off."

Ash kneels and tugs at Ro's flats, and Ro lets her pull them off with one brief, hideous thought about whether her feet might be sweaty and smelly. She can't tell; they're quite simply too far away. Her brain can hardly keep up with what's directly in front of her eyes. She shouldn't be this drunk — she has never been this drunk — but the world is a spinning blur, and she can't finish a thought.

"Do you have anything important happening tomorrow?" Ash asks her.

Ro blinks, trying to remember how time works. "Monday. Class at one."

"Then I'll wake you up at ten. Will that suit?"

"I'm an idiot," is all Ro can say.

"If you were an idiot, I wouldn't be drawn to you," Ash whispers in Ro's ear as she pulls the covers up over her, folding them down around her. "Now sleep."

Ash leans down to kiss her on the forehead and Ro rises up, eyes closed, her body reaching for the touch of those lips like a flower aching for the sun. When she opens her eyes, Ash is gone. The room is pitch dark but for a seam of light under the door.

Ro tries to settle in, but she's never been able to sleep in jeans. She pats down her pockets but doesn't find her phone. She must have left it outside, maybe on the swing. She shimmies out of her pants and lets them drop to the floor, and then becomes painfully aware of the underwire in her bra. Soon she's naked but for her panties — cute ones the color of azalea blooms. Part of her recognizes that this is very strange, being nearly naked in Ash's childhood bed, but the rest of her is just grateful to be free of all the constricting fabrics so she can finally fall unconscious.

She feels very, very wrong, but before that, she felt so deliciously right. She doesn't know how this happened, and she can't stop it. She can only succumb.

9

R o does not sleep well; she never does after excess alcohol. She has bright bursts of dreams and nightmares that fade as she briefly wakes, groggy and breathing hard, like she's been running. Sometimes she is too cold and reaches for covers that aren't there, and sometimes she's too hot and claws away the thick, suffocating quilt. The night feels as if it lasts for days. She imagines Ash sitting on the rocking chair in the dark, watching her with the bright, unblinking eyes of a hawk. There's a growing pain roiling in her belly. In her dreams she's pregnant with some sort of great snake, and she startles to fully awake and bolts out of bed, throwing open the door and barely making it to the hallway bathroom before she's on her knees before the toilet, naked and shaking, learning that Ash's good food doesn't taste so delicious coming back up. She hasn't vomited this violently since she was a kid, and she's painfully aware that Ash has to know what's going on, because it's horribly loud in a silent house. The first break she gets, she flushes and shuts the door, grateful that Ash didn't see her like this when it was beyond her abilities to stop it.

She enters some sort of fugue state, half awake and half asleep, reaching consciousness only when the next wave is coming. It isn't pretty, but there's a perverse interest in watching what comes up. The worst is the tapenade — tasting it again, and then having to see it, the little rubbery squares of green and gray. Again and again she's up and then down, trying to get comfortable when there is no comfort. She looks longingly at Ash's fluffy white towel but refuses to touch it when she's this gruesome.

She wakes on her side, her feverish skin plastered to the tiles. Apparently, even in the midst of channeling sickness from hell itself, she was polite enough to move the rag rug away. She flushes and sips water directly from the tap and peeks out between the open blinds to see that it is dawn.

Maybe Ash isn't awake.

Maybe she sleeps hard.

Maybe she doesn't know.

Ro isn't sure what would be more embarrassing, being caught jogging naked back to her room or having to admit that she thinks Ash's cooking might have given her food poisoning. She had a lot to drink, but not that much, not enough to cause this sort of digestive pyrotechnics — not in someone of her age and size. She's not usually a puker; her body is happy enough to hold its drink.

And yet.

She throws up again, mostly dry heaves and the small amount of water she sipped from the sink, plus a few glistening gray cubes of tapenade. There's a knock at the door, and she goes still.

"Yes?" Ro croaks.

"Are you okay?"

A guilty flush. "I don't know how to answer that."

"Is there anything I can do?"

"Um, don't watch my sprint of shame as I return to your spare room to get my clothes?"

A fond giggle. "I'll go take care of the chickens. And fix you a hangover cure."

"That sounds ominous."

"Well, look at it this way — could you possibly feel worse?"

Ro snorts. "No, I don't think I could."

"Well, then."

Ro stands on shaking legs and looks in the oval mirror. A spray of red freckles covers her cheeks — petechiae, she knows — and one of her eyes is bloodshot from the pressure of all that puking. Her hair is sweaty and limp, her skin goosebumped and clammy. She does not want Ash to see her this way.

"Is it okay if I take a shower?" she asks.

There is no answer. Ash must have gone to take care of the chickens. She takes that as a no.

Ro splashes her face with water and washes her hands, but the gardenia scent feels sickly and aggressive now. She stands at the door and calls Ash's name, but there's no answer. With a prayer to any gods actively listening, she throws open the door and darts down the hall and into the spare room, shutting and locking the door. As she gets dressed, she feels hideous, dirty, contemptible, as if the beautiful ballerina in the framed print is disgusted with her. She didn't want Ash to see her naked, but she doesn't really want her to see her clothed just now, either. This is not the accurate but carefully curated version of herself she's taken care to present thus far. She's certain she does not smell good. She won't feel comfortable again until she's had a long, hot, hard shower with lots of soap and is wearing clean clothes with her wet hair up in a bun.

Dressed now, she takes pains to make Ash's guest bed look nice, even though she's quite certain the sweat-damp sheets will need washing. On second thought, she strips off the sheets, finding a big, strange stain in the center of the mattress, the faded brown of old blood — maybe from an especially bad period leak. Poor little Ash. She pulls the quilt over it neatly and sits at the foot of the bed and looks around, recalling that this was Ash's room as a child. It definitely doesn't look like a child's bedroom, but then again Ash probably put her old toys up in the attic or something; she isn't duty bound to leave her dolls and stuffed animals stacked up on the window seat. Still, outside of the ballerina, there is nothing here that tells a story, no shelf of books, no broken jewelry box, no posters or — well, what would a kid have in their room, if they were raised without TV? Maybe she didn't even have toys. Maybe in the attic there's a wooden rocking horse and a stick and hoop.

This is an adult woman's guest room, a bed and a dresser and an old rocking chair, and Ro can sit here as long as she likes and still not learn anything else. If she's honest with herself, she's only prolonging the inevitable. She might as well go out there and get it over with before she's tempted to break her promise and open the closet or the dresser drawers to glean any facts she can about the girl Ash once was.

She stands, slips on her flats, and goes out to face the music.

The scent hits her first — breakfast.

She's half ravenous, half nauseated.

Ash is in the kitchen in a long cotton nightgown with her apron over the top and her hair up in a messy bun. She's barefoot and humming to herself, and it's the most beautiful thing Ro has ever seen.

"Sorry about that," she begins.

Ash turns to her with a gentle smile and an old percolator in her hand. "Nothing to be sorry about. Sit down and drink that."

She points to a tall glass of orange juice on the table. Ro feels as if she's been offered a reprieve, so she obediently sits and takes a sip.

"Drink it all down, fast," Ash says.

Ro doesn't want to drink all of anything, especially not fast, but she has done something horrible in Ash's bathroom and Ash has heard it and probably smelled it, so Ro will do anything she asks, even if it sounds like a terrible idea. She gulps all the orange juice down, noting a strangely salty taste and a globular texture, and then realizing too late that she has just swallowed a raw egg.

She splutters and dabs at her mouth with a napkin. "Was that an egg?"

Ash nods. "Best hangover cure there is. Freshly squeezed orange juice, salt, and an egg. You'll feel better in no time."

Ro does not believe that. She feels worse.

So much worse.

She's not going to make it to the bathroom.

She runs to the sink, shouts, "I'm sorry!" and then has to taste the orange juice all over again. Ash holds her hair back and rubs her shoulder until she's done. "I'm so, so sorry," Ro moans. "I'm not usually like this. This is a disaster."

"It's not a disaster. I had a great time last night. I'm just sorry you're feeling so terrible right now. Do you think it might be a bug?" Ash already has a glass of water ready for her, and Ro rinses her mouth out and spits before running the faucet to get rid of the evidence.

"I guess so. The undergrads are disease vectors."

A bug.

That must be it.

There is no world in which she questions Ash's cooking or the freshness of her ingredients.

Plus, Ash doesn't appear sick at all, so it couldn't be the food.

"I should get home and let you return to a life without regurgitation. I don't want you to see me like this."

"Vulnerable?" Ash asks, her hand on Ro's back.

"Loathsome. I don't mind being vulnerable, but I'd rather not smell like a dumpster."

Ash laughs lightly but does not deny it. "Can I pack you a plate? My grandmother said no one should ever leave the house empty handed."

"That would be lovely," Ro says, knowing full well she won't be eating it.

As Ash goes through the fridge, Ro uses a paper towel to wipe off her mouth and goes to throw it in the trash can under the sink. Much to her surprise, she sees a familiar twig, rock, and cluster of leaves among orange peels and egg shells. But where is the snail? Surely Ash didn't throw it away. Maybe it died overnight and she didn't want Ro to know, or maybe Ash released it outside and saved the jar.

Ro's not going to mention the snail. She is going to get out of this house with whatever dignity and mystery she can muster, go home, get clean, and pray that the next time they see each other, Ash won't look at her the way she looks at Jessie. Like she's garbage.

By the time Ash backs out of the fridge, Ro has closed the trash cabinet and is gazing out the window at the garden. It's a gray day that promises rain, and she wants nothing more in all the world than to curl up in her own bed in her cozy pajamas and sleep away the discomfort and embarrassment of the last twelve hours.

"Here. A little bit of everything." Ash hands her a ceramic plate piled high and secured with plastic wrap, plus an old seafoam-green Tupperware container full of pie. "On my dishes, so you have to come back."

Ro momentarily sags with relief to know that she's still in the game. She takes the plate and Tupperware, thanks Ash for a wonderful night, apologizes multiple times, and heads for the door.

"When can I see you again?" Ash asks.

Ro stops and turns, knowing full well her face is shining with hope like a full moon after a storm. Considering the odors and noises she's contributed to the sleepy farmhouse this morning, she is stunned that Ash can stand to be in her presence. "Whenever you like, if I'm not in class. I don't have a lot going on. I'm in a bit of a new-city, broken-hearted, post-grad-school malaise, if I'm honest."

"We could go for a hike on Wednesday evening, maybe? There are some nice trails near the farmers' market."

An inspired idea. No eating, no drinking, but plenty of being alone.

"Sounds perfect. I'm open any time after four."

"I'll call you." A gasp. "Oh, wait! Don't forget your phone. You left it on the table."

Ro sees it there and sets down her leftovers so she can shove it in her pocket. This is probably the longest she's gone without looking at it in years.

"Thanks. Can't call me if I don't have a phone. Oh, wait. You need my number."

Ash grins sheepishly. "I already star-sixty-nine'd it."

"Ooh. You know the old magic."

For a long moment, they just stand there, and if she weren't a vomit fountain, Ro is fairly certain now would be when they kissed. But — well, no one wants that. She can't even brush her teeth.

"Thanks again," she says, hefting her plastic-wrapped packages. "For everything. I had a marvelous time."

"So did I. Thanks for coming over."

Ro tilts her head in thanks and heads outside. The remains of the charcuterie board have been plundered by some local creature, the wood board on the porch floor and the butter knives splayed out like murder weapons. There's a messy spot where Ash killed the raccoon, the blood gone brownish black. A lone hen pecks at it, and there's a poetry there.

All the way home, Ro doesn't sing. Last night — it was the best of times, it was the worst of times. The highest highs, the lowest lows. If only she hadn't eaten too much, drank too much. Or if only she hadn't had a stomach bug, or whatever that was. She's a professor; her students cough on her constantly, and she has to handle their greasy papers, as she edits best on hard copy and refuses to deal with the slipperiness of late emails. A stomach bug makes sense. After all, Ash ate the exact same food, drank the exact same alcohol, and she wasn't sick at all. She was fresh and blooming, beautiful as the morning. Hopefully Ro didn't give her any germs from that one, perfect kiss before everything went pear shaped.

"I'm a swamp hag," Ro mumbles to herself.

Back home, she lets her department head know she's got a stomach virus and emails all her students and posts the day's work on the class Slack. She showers and puts on her coziest pajamas and falls into bed with *Jane Eyre* playing on the TV and Anon curled up and purring by her side. She dreams of a dead raccoon rotting on a hill of compost. Snails with shells the color of orange juice crawl over its rotting flesh, their soft, wet bodies the greenish gray of tapenade.

When she wakes up that afternoon, her mouth tastes like death and she guiltily throws Ash's food in the garbage.

❧ 10 ❧

The rest of Monday is a blur. By dinner, Ro is well enough to eat lightly buttered toast.

Tuesday is endless, and she feels back to normal. She goes to campus, powers through her lecture, and spends a few hours in the library working on her book, keeping an eye out for Jessie all along. By dinner, she can eat regular food again. She's lost two pounds.

Wednesday is the day of the hike, and Ro feels like she did when she was six and still thought she might wake up on her birthday to find a pony tied to a tree in the yard, back when she was small enough to still believe in magic.

She's so buoyant in class that one of her students, a lackadaisical athlete who's happy with Cs, asks her if she's high.

"I'm high on life, Brayden," she tells him.

After class, she sits in her office for an interminable hour, knowing full well that even though no one has ever shown up for office hours unless they've just flunked a test, if she tries to leave early, someone will immediately appear. The moment her phone clock says 3:30, she's locking her door and practically skipping out to the car. Ash left her a voicemail on Tuesday during class, telling her the name and address of the park, along with directions to get there. It's utterly adorable how Ash doesn't think like a modern person with a pocket computer but like a grandmother who tells someone to turn right at the big tree. Ro uses her map app anyway.

It's a pretty drive to the trails, and Ash is there already, sitting on the tailgate of the old blue truck Ro saw in her yard. She's wearing aesthetically ragged cutoffs and her usual brown leather boots with a white camisole, her hair in French-braid pigtails. Ro is wearing almost the same thing, but her shorts are a bit longer and her camisole is moss green.

"Need bug spray?" Ash asks as Ro gets out of her car bearing gifts: a clean platter and Tupperware, and the tea towel from that first loaf of bread.

"Yes, thanks."

They trade. Ash takes back her things and hands Ro — of course — a spray bottle of clear liquid that is clearly homemade. She sprays it on her legs and arms, and it's as much a perfume as a repellent.

"Smells wonderful," she says as she hands it back.

Ash smiles. "It works, too." She puts the bottle back in her truck. "The trail is about three miles. Is that good for you?"

Ro nods. "Perfect."

Of course, she already knows how long the trail is because she rigorously researches everything and hates being caught unaware or without a plan. She also really likes that Ash asked her if it was okay; she dated a guy in undergrad who invited her for a hike that ended up being seven grueling miles of scrambling over slick rocks and down rooty hills. That relationship did not last long. She couldn't keep up with him on foot; he couldn't keep up with her mind. He later changed majors to become a park ranger.

Ash sets the pace, and Ro walks beside her when there's room and behind her when there isn't. The forest is beautiful, the trail following along a gentle river the color of hazel eyes hiding behind mountain laurels. Ash names paw-paw trees and spicebush and trilliums, points out softshell turtles sunning on the bank, a woodpecker on a dead tree, the footprints of a possum captured in the soft soil of the riverbank. Ro likes this — likes that Ash notices things. She is used to being the only person who notices things.

They pass through a sunny field, and Ash makes a beeline for wild blackberry bushes laden with ripening fruit.

"Is it safe to eat?" Ro asks.

"Why wouldn't it be?"

"Poison, animals, legalities..."

Ash laughs. "They're just blackberries. They can't hurt you."

She plucks a fat berry and holds it out, and Ro pauses for only a moment before opening her mouth to accept it. It tastes like summer incarnate, juicy and tart and sweet, and they spend some time plucking berries and feeding each other the best ones. It's a strange intimacy, but Ro is happy. She often finds herself outside the present moment, and she's doing it now as if already combing through the day's happenings back home in bed. This will be a core memory for her, this moment of laughter in the sun and hot berry juice in the corners of her mouth. They are in a public park but all alone in the world. There was only one other car in the parking lot, and they haven't seen a single soul.

Ash must feel it, too. She puts a berry delicately between her teeth and turns to Ro, her blue eyes daring. Shivering in the sunshine, breath caught, Ro leans in to take the berry into her mouth. Ash doesn't let it go immediately, makes Ro tug it away, their lips meeting as she finally claims her prize.

This may be the hottest thing that has ever happened to her. Ash pulls away and Ro chews the berry, swallows it, and licks her lips. Ash raises her eyebrows teasingly, expectantly, silvery glimmers under the sun's pressing heat. Ro is uncertain, feels like she's lost in a strange land, but she plucks a berry and takes it between her teeth, and warmth pools in her belly as Ash leans in and runs her tongue around the berry, tracing Ro's lips, slipping into her mouth all hot and wet to lick the berry away like a hungry kitten. Ro's legs are weak, her body awake, her hands hungry.

Ash plucks the next berry and moves in with it nestled between rosy lips, grasping Ro's jaw gently in both hands. As Ro opens her mouth, Ash pushes in the berry with her tongue and...dear God, moves it around Ro's mouth like she's chasing it, leaving a trail of slick heat that slithers through Ro's body. Ro tilts her head and plays along, their tongues licking and pushing and pulling until Ash finally pulls away, leaving Ro with the berry.

"Swallow it," Ash says, looking directly and unashamedly at her mouth.

Ro does. Oh, she does.

And then Ash is kissing her for real, and the world falls away because there is nothing in the world except their mouths and their bodies and the sun and the scent of summer among the blackberry bushes, the bees buzzing around them and the birds singing a love song overhead. Ro has never felt this way. It's like drowning but good, like being drunk but awake, like there is no place but where they touch.

Without warning, Ash pulls away completely. Ro blinks like she's waking up, her hands empty, her mouth tasting of blackberries. Why did Ash — Oh.

Ro follows her line of sight. There is a man where there should be no man.

Her body shudders involuntarily, a rabbit in a passing shadow.

He's trying not to be seen, this man, standing still just within the confines of the forest, hiding in the shadows. He is holding his phone up, obviously recording, and the moment he sees them both looking at him, he puts the phone away.

Ro's body is stiff, her face burning.

She doesn't feel safe anymore.

"You," Ash calls, low and angry as she strides toward him.

Oh no.

Oh no oh no oh no.

The guy puts his hands up, backs away looking mortified. He's in his thirties, maybe, pale white and dorky, and has that skinny-fat look to him. "Sorry, I was, uh, checking my — "

"Bullshit. Show me your phone."

The guy looks all around as if hoping someone will save him, but there is nothing here but a field, two flush-faced girls, and a blackberry bush.

Exactly as she might expect, the guy turns around and runs.

Unexpectedly, Ash takes off after him.

Uncertain what to do, Ro follows.

Running is not her strong suit, but apparently either the guy shares her tendency toward exercise-induced asthma or didn't think anyone would actually chase him. There's a grunt as his body slams into the dirt. Ro catches up, and he's on his belly now, Ash standing over him, and Ro doesn't know if Ash pushed him or he tripped and fell on his own. His phone and keys lie on the ground, just out of reach. Ash snatches the phone up, tries to unlock it, and sighs in annoyance. Ro is frozen, watching the scene play out.

"What's your password?" Ash asks him.

"I'm not telling you that." As he attempts to stand up, she holds the phone in front of his face to unlock it, and he shouts, "Hey, no!"

Ash steps away from him, backing up, smiling wickedly, poking at the screen. For someone who doesn't have a phone of her own, she seems to know exactly what she's doing and doesn't seem confused in the slightest.

The guy stands and advances on her, and for a man who didn't appear particularly menacing at first, his anger lends him an air of unpredictable danger that makes Ro's heart rate jack up and her feet ready to run for real. He's taller than Ash and probably has fifty pounds on her, but she doesn't even look up from his phone.

"There. I deleted all your pics and videos. You're a disgusting little freak."

"Give it back," the guy says warningly. "Now."

"No." Ash drops the phone, steps on it hard, and lobs it into the middle of the river, where it disappears with a friendly plop.

"What the fuck, bitch?" the guy spits, jogging to the river's edge and dancing back and forth like he's thinking about going in after it.

When he turns back to Ash with murder in his eyes, she sneers. "Cry about it." She kneels to scoop up his keys and throws them into the river, too. The guy goggles at her, furious but unable to process the fact that someone has stood up to him.

Ash holds out her hand to Ro, and Ro is numb and frozen but manages to take it and let Ash lead her away.

"Don't you fucking dare leave." The guy rushes up behind them, and Ash spins around, putting herself between him and Ro.

"Or what? What are you going to do? Tell the police I destroyed a phone full of pics of underage girls at the pool? Give me a little lecture about privacy? Hit me? What? What are you going to do?"

Ro can't see Ash's face, but she can see the tension in her body, her hands in fists, her feet spread as if she's ready to fight.

And she can see the guy's face flounder as he realizes that if Ash can't be cowed, he has no power over her. He's clearly no fighter, this man. His eyes dart from the river to Ash to the trail as he runs the calculations on his options and finds no good answer.

Ash sees it too. "That's what I thought. Now we're going to leave, and if you follow us, I will fuck you up. Got it?"

The guy snorts and shakes his head and calls her a bitch under his breath as he turns away in the universal sign of a loser recognizing that he's lost. Ash turns and takes Ro's hand again, giving her an encouraging smile.

"Don't worry," she says softly in an entirely different voice. "It's over. He won't bother us again."

Ro can only nod. Her body is still in fight–flight–freeze mode. Angry men do that to her. She is numb and stupid. As Ash leads her down the trail, she doesn't even look back to make sure the guy isn't following them. They pass the blackberry bushes and continue through the field, to where the trail forks into three different directions. Ash chooses one that takes them away from the river and up some big rocks.

"Are you okay to climb?" Ash asks.

Ro nods. She can only nod. For once, she doesn't have words.

The trail zigs and zags upward, and they scramble up the big rocks, sometimes using trees and roots for leverage. Ash leads the way, constantly looking back to make sure Ro is still with her and not having trouble — and looking beyond her to make sure the guy hasn't decided to follow them. They finally emerge on a big, flat rock high over the river. Ash sits near the edge and pats the stone beside her, and Ro creeps forward and obediently collapses.

It's very pretty, but her gaze is unfocused.

"That scared you, huh?" Ash asks gently.

Ro, again, nods. Her lips twitch and she tries to speak a few times before she manages to find the right word. "Yes."

"Okay." Ash turns to her, sitting cross-legged. "It's like you're an animal caught in a trap. Your body is telling you to either run, fight, or freeze. What feels right?"

"I feel frozen. I'm a freezer. I freeze."

"So you're an antelope caught by a lion, holding very, very still so it will think you're dead and it will relax its grip. What do you do the moment it loses interest and walks away?"

"Get up and run."

Ash nods and smiles. "Good. So jump up and run. Push the lion away. Scream. You need to dissipate that energy."

Ro looks down, feels her cheeks redden. "I would feel silly."

"Who cares? That guy is gone. It's just you, me, and the forest. No one else."

"But I can't run. We're on a rock."

A chuckle. "Look, bodies are kind of dumb. Your body doesn't know the difference between actually sprinting away from a lion and jogging in place. Wave your arms, dance around — whatever gets the energy out so you're not frozen anymore. I'll look away, if you like."

Ro nods. This makes sense. She heard about this on a self-help podcast once. She stands up, and when Ash looks away, she moves closer to where the big rock emerges from the ground and shakes out her hands and feet. That helps a little — she can feel the blood flow returning. Letting herself think about the man, about the way he made her feel, she runs in place, gives a few experimental jumps, and then pushes the air away in a big gesture as she shouts, "No!"

The effect is almost immediate, like a full-body sigh.

She goes back to sit beside Ash.

"You were right."

"I'm always right." Ash puts a hand on her knee.

Ro turns to her, drinking in her profile, the slope of her perfect nose, the spray of freckles she wants to cover with kisses. "Where'd you learn that?"

"I wasn't always screen free. A while back, I took some online psychology courses. Didn't want to go away to college, knew I didn't need the degree, but I like learning."

Ro melts a little inside. This might be the most attractive thing she's ever heard. "You weren't even scared of that guy," she says.

Ash squeezes her knee. "He's a coward. Guys like that always are."

Ro looks down and barges ahead because she has to know. "Have you ever dated one?"

"What, a coward?"

Ro bumps Ash's shoulder with her own. "No. A guy."

A sigh. "I've tried. Let's just say they're not really to my taste."

"But that punk guy at the farmers' market…" Ro can hear it the moment it comes out of her mouth, how nosy and obsessed it sounds.

116

But Ash just laughs. "I'm a salesman. I have to sell product. You'd be amazed what a big smile and a little bounce can do to a man's shopping basket. Now, how about you? Besides your ex, was it all guys?"""

"It's been all guys. Until…" Ro trails off.

"Until this," Ash finishes for her. She reaches over and grabs Ro's hand, giving it a squeeze and dragging it over to rest on her knee.

Suddenly shy, Ro can only stare at their hands, even though she knows Ash is looking at her and wants her to look back. There is a gravity to this — to them — that she hasn't experienced before. A realness, a vulnerability, a…question. With guys, there was an unspoken understanding that they were out for sex and would push and needle and nudge for every inch of skin they could conquer. Even the shy ones, even the sweet ones, wanted something of her that she wasn't always willing to give but knew was expected of her. It was like constantly ceding land to a country with a more powerful army. She always knew she would be left with less than she originally possessed.

But with Ash, here, now, thus far, even if Ro constantly feels shy and silly, it's more a meeting of equals, and Ro doesn't know what to do with that. She doesn't know what's required of her. After all, men are expected to lead the dance while women follow. But with two women, and one just learning about this side of herself, who will even choose the music?

This isn't a land war — this is undiscovered country.

"Are you scared of me now?" Ash asks softly.

That gets Ro's attention. "Scared of you? Why? How?" She shakes her head as if this thought is too silly to consider. "Never."

"Well, the raccoon made you uncomfortable. And I was pretty brutal with that guy..."

"With the pervert who was taking creepy videos of us and then threatened you? He deserved worse than that. Wait. Do you think he saved that stuff to the cloud?"

Ash laughs. "Nope. I wiped it."

Ro looks at her. "How'd you know how?"

Because Ro can barely find the iCloud on her own phone, which she uses constantly. There's no way a borderline Amish person could figure that out in the sixty seconds Ash had that guy's phone.

The look Ash gives her is sharp, probing. "I told you, I wasn't always screen free. I went through a rebellious phase when I was younger, right after my grandmother passed. I did everything she'd told me not to. Full dive into technology. Got the latest iPhone, a laptop, a TV. Made moonshine. Grew some weed. Joined online dating sites. Met some guys. Met some girls. Realized she'd been right all along — technology didn't make me any happier. So I got rid of most of it but kept what I needed."

Chastened, Ro rubs her thumb over the back of Ash's hand. "Oh. That makes sense."

"Everything I do makes sense. Anything else bothering you?"

Ro scoots a little closer, leans her head on Ash's shoulder. "It's been an irrational sort of day. I hate conflict. That guy scared me. I was scared for you."

Ash leans her head against Ro's, and Ro can smell her shampoo.

Roses, always roses.

"You don't need to be scared for me. That guy was weak, inside and out. And even if he tried something, I wasn't raised to go out into the middle of nowhere unprotected." Ash pulls something out of her pocket and reveals a jagged little black handle that flicks out to show a vicious blade. "My grandmother taught me not to walk in the woods alone unless I was certain I was the most dangerous thing there."

"You've had that on you the whole time?"

"It's a farm thing. I always have a knife on me. There's baling twine, annoying vines, flowers that need cutting, fruit that needs eating, chickens that always seem to get tangled in old fishing line."

Ro knows almost nothing about knives, other than how often they're used in Shakespeare. She tentatively reaches out to press her thumb against the blade and is somehow surprised to discover how sharp it is.

"Ow!"

Ash pulls away, snaps the blade shut, and shoves it back in her pocket. She turns to Ro, and gently takes her hand, holding up her thumb to show a single bead of blood.

"That was surprisingly unwise, for you," Ash says. "But you'll live."

"I'm very stupid after my amygdala kicks in," Ro admits. "I didn't think it was that sharp."

"Dull knives are dangerous. Come here, you little fool."

Ash turns Ro to face her, knee to knee, and pulls Ro's hand toward her and slips Ro's thumb into her mouth. Ro is shocked at the effect this has on the rest of her body. She has forgotten the brief, hot pain of the blade's tip, the sensation lost in the soft, wet heat of a girl's mouth and the gentle caress of her tongue. When Ash releases her thumb, she drags her lips down it in a suggestive way that makes Ro realize possibly why men are such sex pests. She wants things she's never had before, things she can't describe, and she wants them here with Ash, right now, please.

"There. All better. Don't do that again."

Ro swallows hard. "No promises."

There's a subtle shift in Ash, like the weather changing, that sudden fall of heavy clouds that eclipses a merry sun. Her gaze darkens as her hands move from Ro's knees to her thighs, slip up to slide her thumbs in the creases of her hips.

"Do you want me to kiss you?" she asks, voice husky.

"Yes."

"Do you want me to be gentle or rough?"

No one has ever asked Ro this question before.

"Rough but not painful," she says softly.

Ash smiles.

It's as if the entire forest goes silent and still as Ash rises to her knees, puts a hand behind Ro's head, and kisses her with a gentle pressure that forces her, inch by inch, onto her back on the stone. It's warm from the sun, hard and craggy, and Ro tries to shift to a comfortable spot and fails. It doesn't matter. Ash is the sun now, eclipsing everything.

The kiss is rough and decidedly not painful. Ash drags a knee up between Ro's legs and murmurs, "Say no any time you want me to stop."

In response, Ro winds her leg over Ash's calf and kisses her back.

Time stands still. Ro feels like the soft, hot earth breaking open under a plow. Everything is new and yet familiar, hard but tender, surprising and yet exactly what she expected the first time Ash's lips touched hers. She's gaining confidence, realizes that she is an active participant, and begins to explore. She has made out before, but not like this, not with this willingness, this openness, this curiosity.

But when Ash flicks open the button on her jean shorts, Ro gasps and tenses up.

"No?" Ash says, lips plump from kissing.

"Not here. Not after that guy."

Ash looks up the hill into the forest like she's going to spot him lurking behind a tree, but there is no one there. "Another time, then. Another place."

"I'd like that."

Ro sits up and is immediately dizzy. There is no blood in her head. She feels like she's just lived through an earthquake. She buttons her shorts, rearranges her bra and shirt, smooths back her hair, puts a hand to her lips.

"Wow," she breathes.

Ash gives her a fond look. "Wow indeed." She stands smoothly and pulls Ro up, and then they're back on the trail as if nothing ever happened, as if Ro's entire world wasn't just turned upside down.

At least her earlier fear and apprehension are gone, washed away in a torrent of far more potent chemicals. She can only think of Ash — her lips, her eyes, her hands, oh her hands. Even the little cut on her thumb no longer hurts. Whatever possessed her to put her thumb against a knife's tip...Well, she's not currently thinking with her logical mind.

They pass no one as they head back the way they came. Ro keeps waiting for the creepy guy to jump out from behind a tree and...she doesn't even know. Threaten them? He's in the only car in the parking lot, which is decidedly not running, and Ro wonders if they should take photos of the plates just in case. But Ash grabs her hand, entwining their fingers, and spins her like they're dancing.

"He won't bother us. Ignore him."

"I'm trying."

Ash pulls her close. "Focus on me. That was fun, wasn't it?"

"It really was. Creepers notwithstanding."

Ash's eyes narrow as she looks back toward his car. Surely he's seen them, but he's not getting out. "If he even tries to talk to me again..."

"Well, at least you already gave him what he deserved."

"He deserves much worse."

Now it's Ro's turn to grab Ash's hand and pull her back into the moment. "Hey. I'm here. We got through it. You were magnificent. I've never been that brave around misbehaving men."

"The stuff on his phone, though! Disgusting."

"And you destroyed it and chased him off. And now we can just forget he ever existed and focus on better things. Yes?" She

grabs Ash's other hand, pulls her close, and just…drinks her in.
When she looks at Ash, she feels radiant, glowing, open. As she
watches, Ash leaves her dark rage and meets Ro in this space
they've created for themselves, this warm little bubble.

"Yes," Ash grudgingly admits.

"Want to grab dinner? Do you like poke?"

Annoyance flashes in Ash's eyes. "I don't like restaurants.
I don't know where the meat comes from, or how it's cooked.
Factory farming makes me sick. I'd cook for you, but I don't have
anything fresh, or even defrosted."

Ro squeezes her hands. "I can live on a cheese plate. Want
to come to my house?"

"I'd prefer mine."

"Look, I don't care where we are. I just want to spend more
time with you."

At that, Ash thaws again. She's like her own weather system,
Ro is learning. Sure, most people are always learning, to some
degree, but maybe she's never paid this much attention before
now. Or maybe she's still on alert after the incident with the
creepy guy. Or maybe women are just different from guys —
more sensitive, more changeable. She's fairly certain that she'll
never ask Ash what she's thinking and hear her dully say,
"Nothing," and mean it.

Ro doesn't mind. She's enjoying the dance. She's not on
autopilot. She's wide awake. It's refreshing. They form a plan
in which they'll both go home and get cleaned up, and Ro will
stop by the store for fruit while Ash supplies the cheese and
charcuterie. Ash asks if she wants to bring wine, but Ro shakes

her head firmly. She won't be drinking like that again; she can't afford to miss more work. Sure, she could have one nice glass, but she has trouble saying no to Ash, and if Ash pours her another drink, she knows she'll take it. She'll be at Ash's house at eight.

As she turns on her music and waits to turn out of the parking lot, she looks back and notices that Ash hasn't left yet. She's just sitting in her truck. She doesn't have a phone, so it's not like she's doing the usual thing and catching up on email and social. That guy is still in his car, too, and it makes Ro nervous, leaving Ash alone with him around. If she had a cell phone, Ro would text her to check in, but instead, she backs up, turns around, and pulls in next to Ash.

When she rolls down her window, Ash gives her a look of slight frustration. "What's wrong?"

"I was just worried about you being alone in the parking lot with that creep," Ro admits. "Do you want me to wait for you?"

That little V appears between Ash's eyebrows. "No. I'm just writing something down." She holds up a small notebook. "You go ahead. I'm not worried about him."

"Are you sure?"

The little V turns into a full-blown frown that makes Ro shrink back.

"Remember when we talked about boundaries? I need space, too. I don't respond well to being nagged or mothered. If I tell you I'm okay, I'm okay, and you have to trust me. Okay?"

"Okay," Ro says, because that's her only option.

Ash smiles again. "Good. Now go on. I wouldn't want you to be late for our date."

Ro blows her a kiss and drives off. Waiting to turn onto the main road, she looks back at Ash's truck and feels exactly the same amount of worry as she did before that embarrassing rebuke. If this is going to work, she has to trust that Ash knows what she's doing. Ash has made it abundantly clear that she can take care of herself.

Ro drives off, but she's uneasy. There's so much about Ash that feels like a perfect fit, but there are times Ro doesn't understand her at all.

11

Ro sings all the way home. She had a roommate in undergrad who said she could always tell if Ro was happy or depressed based on whether she was singing. When she's happy, there's always a soundtrack — in the car, while cooking, in the shower — but when she's down, there is only silence. She is suddenly realizing that before meeting Ash she hadn't sung in months, not since she left Erik, but now it just pours out of her. Ash makes her feel like a symphony.

She gets cleaned up and puts on a cute dress she recently ordered online and goes to the fancy grocery store, where she selects tender peaches and hard black grapes, tart apples, and a small watermelon that thumps just right.

It's dark now, the moon high and the stars sparkling as her car swoops up and down the country roads. When Ash's mailbox materializes from the shadows, Ro feels like she's coming home, like something great is going to happen. She hasn't felt this way in years, not since she got into her PhD program at

Columbia — or maybe when she got the offer for her book, before Erik started questioning the size of her admittedly minuscule advance. Even before his betrayal came to light, he had a way of killing her happiness, she's starting to realize. She had mistaken complacency for comfort, had thought that was simply what long-term relationships felt like — like a long, drawn-out surrender. Maybe it doesn't have to feel that way, though, if you're with the right person. Her tires crunch on the dirt, a brown chicken darting away from her headlights, off into the bushes.

The lights aren't on, inside or out, and Ash's truck isn't here. That doesn't seem right, and Ro immediately thinks of the guy in the parking lot and wonders if perhaps Ash was too confident about his weakness. Guilt pecks at her — she should never have left Ash alone there. She wishes more than ever that Ash had a cell phone. She knocks on the door.

There is no answer.

She didn't expect one.

"Ash, you in there?" she calls.

The property is quiet, the leaves rustling in the dark. Soft violin music billows from somewhere in the backyard, offering a bright thread of hope. Maybe Ash parked in the barn? Maybe she's waiting out back, where the music is?

It's a pathetic hope, but Ro hopes nonetheless. Reusable grocery bag in hand, using her phone as a flashlight so she won't trip, Ro follows the stone path into the backyard. At night, with no light, it's a world of shifting shadows. Another chicken darts by, and Ro startles back, remembering the possibly rabid raccoon. She's glad she's wearing boots as she navigates the twisting path. This is no place for bare feet.

The music gets louder, and she's drawn past the chicken coop and the greenhouse to the potting shed. The doors are still thrown open and the grow lights are on, a beacon amidst the darkness. Ro puts down her bag and hunts for the source of the sound, finding an old, cracked iPhone nestled in a corner behind a stack of empty pots, plugged into the wall. She wakes it up to show sheet-music wallpaper, but it's locked. It's a different piece than last time but sounds like the same musician — a violinist of immaculate skill and masterly passion.

But — Ash said she didn't own a phone.

This is a phone.

Maybe she just uses it for the music. Maybe it doesn't have service. The face is too smashed up to use for much, so it's probably from her rebellious patch and she just keeps it around to help the plants grow. Ro puts it back carefully, exactly as she found it, and backs out of the shed, feeling as if she's trespassing.

She heads out toward the barn, passing two tall boxes that she doesn't recognize as beehives until she can hear their sleepy thrum. The barn is a big thing, two stories and well kept for a building that's clearly ancient. There are no windows that she can find, and the double doors sport a shiny silver padlock. Now that she's back here, Ro can see that there's no way Ash could park near the barn — the yard is a labyrinth of bushes and waist-high raised beds full of looming, nodding plants. She suddenly feels very far from the house, very far from anything familiar.

She hurries back toward the safety of the front porch but stops when she notices a terrible odor emanating from the side of the house she hasn't seen yet.

There's the compost pile, made out of old pallets and stacked high with eggshell-speckled black dirt and a pitchfork nearby to turn it. Then three big garbage cans, unmarked. Seems like a lot of trash cans for just one girl who claims never to waste anything — but then again, Ash is running a business and likely creates a lot of recycling and garbage. Ro is just reaching to open the first can when she hears Ash's truck turn at the mailbox. She hurries around front and is standing on the porch, slightly out of breath, when Ash's headlights slide over her.

When Ash exits the car, she looks exhausted and is still in her clothes from the hike.

"Are you okay?" Ro asks her. "Was it the creeper guy? Did he hurt you?"

Shaking her head, Ash pulls out a key ring and unlocks the door. "Dropped my keys in the forest and had to go back and find them. The guy didn't bother me at all, but I'm starving after all that hiking. I have never been more excited about a cheese plate."

Ro is flooded with guilt and concern. "Why didn't you tell me? I could've helped you look for them. Or brought you home for a spare."

"The truck was unlocked, so I didn't realize until you were already gone. Not a big deal." Ash opens the door and hits the light switch before giving Ro a mischievous grin. "Besides, now I have to get clean. Want to join me?"

"I already — oh. *Oh.* Okay."

The mood has changed utterly.

Ash takes the bag of fruit from Ro and puts it in the fridge before taking Ro's hand and leading her through the dark house, past the mysterious door, to the big bedroom. Ro follows shyly, her cheeks warm. There is random and unexpected making out in a forest, and then there is this new, willful, brazen intimacy of a proposed shared bathing experience.

Ash turns on a lamp by the door and sits Ro on her high brass bed. "Wait here a moment." She's halfway to the bathroom before she says, "I forgot something..." She reaches into a drawer and pulls out a black satin sleep mask. "Is this okay?"

"Yes. I like that you ask. Let's just assume from here on out that I'll tell you if something isn't working for me, and you do the same. Okay?"

Ash smiles. "Okay." She takes a brush from the nightstand drawer and sits behind Ro on the bed, brushing her hair in long, sensual strokes. Ro closes her eyes and allows herself to enjoy the sensation. No one has brushed her hair since she was little and her mother ripped through her tangles after a shower. This is different. This is meant to feel nice.

It does.

She sighs like a cat in a sunbeam.

Once her hair is smooth, Ash gathers it up into a high bun, twirling it and securing it with a rubber band before slipping on the mask. "Wait here. I'll be back soon."

With the mask over her eyes, Ro can barely see a line of light at her nose but nothing else. Her other senses kick in and she hears water turn on in a tub followed by the shaking sprinkle of salts. The scent of rosemary and lemon kicks in — just like the cupcakes, and she smiles to think that what Ash is doing…it's personal. She's met guys with an MO, who always take girls to the same restaurants and the same dates, but she likes the way Ash is always thinking about what Ro in particular might enjoy.

Next she hears a familiar swish-flick sound and smells fire — Ash is lighting candles. Another nice touch. The scent of beeswax floats in and she remembers that Ash makes the candles herself from her own beeswax. Is there anything she can't do? She's incredible. And for some reason, she likes Ro. Maybe it was the wordplay to start, but Ash must feel the same spark, sense a calling, like to like. Ro is not a child; she knows this is infatuation, knows that her brain is flooding her body with hormones and bonding chemicals. And yet it's so much stronger than it's ever been with anyone else. Ash takes care of her. Ash makes her want to lower her defenses and unfurl like a blowsy peony. Ash makes her want to be soft when everything else in the world conspires to make her hard.

By the time Ash's bare feet patter across the room, Ro is almost vibrating with anticipation. But Ash doesn't take her hand; she unzips Ro's boots and gently slips them off her feet, then her socks. She helps Ro stand and runs a finger down Ro's clavicle.

"Is this — oh. You said it was okay."

Ash is facing her now, and she slips her fingers under both of Ro's straps and tugs them down over her shoulders, peeling the dress down over her bra. Ro shivers as the dress pools around her bare feet.

"Beautiful," Ash murmurs. "So beautiful." She unclasps Ro's bra and gently lifts it off, giving a little hum of pleasure when Ro is revealed.

Ro is glad for the mask. It's easier to let this happen in the darkness, to be stripped bare and seen, really seen. She steps out of her matching panties and is completely naked. As someone who has a complicated relationship with her body, this is a pivotal moment for her. Terrifying. Thrilling. She wants to suck her stomach in but will not play that game with another woman. This is her. This is Ro. Ash can take it or leave it.

"Beautiful," Ash says again, gently kissing the corner of her mouth before taking her hand. "Absolutely perfect."

She leads Ro carefully into the ensuite bathroom and helps her into what feels like an absolutely gigantic clawfoot tub. Ro can't see it, but Ash places her hand on the edge, and she can only imagine that it's exactly what she would expect from Ash so far. The water is hot, just the right temperature, and she sinks in with a sigh. She hasn't felt this cared for since she was twelve and had the flu. She feels rosy and worshipped and delicate as a porcelain cup. She has no idea what is coming, but she can't wait to find out.

The water shifts and sloshes as Ash slips into the tub with her. *Oh*, Ro thinks with a quiver of excitement, *Ash is naked, too*. There's just enough room if they sit knee to knee.

Ash takes Ro's hand and runs a washcloth up her arm, under her arm, down her side. It's so relaxing that Ro wants to lie back and go limp, but it's so sensual that she can feel her skin pucker in the wake of every stroke. She repeats this for Ro's other arm, leaning forward to rub the washcloth in circles over Ro's back. They're so close now that Ro sets her forehead against Ash's neck, breathing in the scent of dried sweat and old rose and that faint woodiness from the hike, plus a faint whiff of something metallic — maybe old truck smell? The washcloth moves around front, down Ro's neck and over her chest, tender and soft yet firm and unafraid in its path. Ro can barely breathe, can feel every place where they touch.

"My turn," Ash murmurs, and Ro feels her body shift as she washes herself.

"Can I help you with that?" she offers, but Ash chuckles.

"No. Let me do all the work. Just relax."

Ro slides down a little, her knees settling against Ash's. She leans her head back over the tub's sloping back and is barely able to peek under the mask and catch tantalizing glimpses of Ash washing. She's less sensuous and more businesslike, her hair up in the same high bun. Ro's eyes wander down, but she doesn't want Ash to catch her sneaking a look. Not now. Not when Ash has forgiven her for snooping.

There's a soft smack as the washcloth is laid over the side of the tub, and then Ash reaches for Ro's hand and spreads her fingers. "Hold still," she murmurs before clipping Ro's fingernails down to the skin. Ro dares a glance and sees dainty silver scissors snip-snip-snipping, and at first she is vaguely annoyed because she took the time to file her nails and paint them a pretty lavender, but then she realizes why two naked women in a bathtub might need to have their nails trimmed and has to wonder if Ash noticed her breathing speed up.

Ash finishes one hand, takes up the next, and then snips her own nails, although Ro knows she keeps them short already. She takes her time, working with the sort of careful precision Ro would expect from someone who makes such flawless cupcakes.

"Oh, an eyelash," Ash says, and Ro feels the brief caress of a single fingertip on her cheek. When she peeks under the mask, she sees Ash place the eyelash on her tongue with her eyes closed and swallow it with a sense of reverence. How odd, Ro thinks, that some small part of her is inside Ash's body right now.

Ash stands, and from under the mask Ro sees...a lot. She is intensely curious about...that...and knows virtually nothing about other women's bodies but assumes, as an intelligent and responsive woman, that she'll figure it out. Ash grabs a towel, dries off, and steps out before helping Ro to stand and enveloping her in a big, fluffy towel that smells like it was dried outside in the sun. It probably was.

Once Ash has tenderly rubbed her dry, she leads Ro to her bed, still blindfolded, and then things get very, very interesting.

12

Sometime later, coated in a sheen of sweat and starving, they head for the kitchen. Ro washes and cuts the fruit while Ash prepares the cheese, meat, butter, and bread and sets out a frosty pitcher of lemonade. If this was at a guy's house, Ro would ask to borrow a T-shirt, but, well, she can't fit into Ash's clothes, and she can't imagine Ash having a drawer full of old 5k shirts. Ash doesn't get dressed, so Ro follows her lead, and it's odd at first, moving about the house in the nude, but...well, they are out in the middle of nowhere. There is no one to peep in the windows, just as there was no one to hear her cry out, again and again. No thin-walled apartment next door, no nosy neighbors, just two bodies going feral by candlelight. Just as with the washing in the tub, Ash did all the work. Every time Ro tried to return the favor, Ash redoubled her efforts. When Ro asked her why, she only said, "Let me do this for you," and Ro had no choice but to acquiesce.

Ro isn't sure how comfortable she would be sitting down on furniture, but they eat standing up at the counter, cutting cheese with the same sharp little knife. They feed each other peach slices and grapes and crisp triangles of watermelon, and when juice runs down Ro's chin, Ash laps it up, trailing from her chest up her throat to her lips. They kiss, and then Ash kneels before her, and…

Yes. It's quite a night.

Once they're done eating — dear God, yes — Ash cleans up the remains of the platter, separating trash from compost from chicken scraps. There's a sparse elegance in her movements, an assertive functionality that Ro finds as beautiful as the very shape of her. She knows now the hidden places where Ash's veins turn periwinkle blue, the ticklish place over her ribs that makes her lurch away, how her pupils blow wide and black in the blue when she's excited. Ro may not have full knowledge of Ash's most private places, but not for lack of trying. She still knows the secret smell of her, the taste of her mouth, the softest place on her thighs. And in turn, Ash has this knowledge of her and more.

"Come to bed," Ash says, padding down the hall, and Ro trails behind, watching Ash's long, golden hair sway over the knobs of her spine.

Ash pulls back the covers of the big bed and lays Ro out like a doll, pulling the quilt up over her. She leaves then, blows out all the bathroom candles, and brushes her teeth. Ro wishes she could do the same, but she's rinsed with enough water and feels particularly shy about asking for anything Ash doesn't outright offer. That's a thing she's noticing about Ash: she likes to be the leader, and when something is suggested that she didn't have planned, she gets that little V between her eyebrows and can't help showing annoyance. Ro assumes it's because Ash lives like a hermit and isn't accustomed to dealing with the needs and whims of others. She can be so generous, but maybe that works best when it's on her terms. It's odd, but it's something that Ro hopes will naturally work itself out.

They fall asleep as spoons, and in the deepest part of night, Ro wakes up to use the bathroom. She is no longer under Ash's arm; Ash is on her side of the bed, curled up around a ragged old scrap of blanket.

"No," Ash mumbles into her pillow. "I didn't do it, I didn't waste, I'll be good. Please, Grandma, please. Don't do it. It's too hot."

Ro gazes at Ash's back, wondering if she should wake her.

But no. This nightmare is personal, and Ro doesn't want to make things awkward between them. Not now.

"It's okay," she says, stroking Ash's shoulder. "You're safe."

At that, Ash goes still.

Quietly, carefully, Ro slips from under the crisp sheet and heavy quilt and squints as she navigates across the room. She closes the bathroom door before fumbling for the light switch and sighs with relief as she pees. She hasn't really seen this room — she was blindfolded, before — and she is grateful for this glimpse into Ash's life without Ash there to watch Ro watching.

It's a spare room, clean and tidy. There's a narrow shower with a frosted-glass door, three hand-labeled glass pump bottles outside suggesting Ash really does like to know where her products come from. Two washrags dry on the tub, dripping onto the waxed-wood floor. Beeswax pillar candles sit on a small table nearby, along with the silver scissors and a tiny clay bowl. When she's done and has flushed and washed her hands, Ro peers into the bowl and sees a little pile of lavender crescent moons — her clipped fingernails. Not Ash's unpainted nails, though — just Ro's. She's puzzled and can't imagine what Ash would want with her nails, why she didn't immediately throw them away, but then again, Ash doesn't waste anything. Maybe they're good for the chickens, or maybe they help the compost. Ro's not going to ask, though. Ash is odd, but she's also clever, fun, delightful, strong, and a deeply attentive and generous lover. The mystery is part of the allure.

"Rosemary?"

"Coming!"

Ro turns off the light and scurries back to bed.

"Where were you?"

"Nature called. Three glasses of lemonade."

She crawls under the covers and Ash pulls her close. "Don't wander," Ash whispers in her ear.

Ash's arm is so tight around her middle that Ro can barely breathe, but she whispers, "I don't. I won't. Just the bathroom."

With a sigh, Ash relaxes. "Good."

13

The next morning, Ro wakes up to Ash nuzzling her ear.

"Like omelets?" Ash asks.

"Like you," Ro responds.

Thirty minutes later, Ash is whipping up hen-warm eggs with a fork while Ro sits at the table. Again she is struck by the simple pleasure of being pampered; she's more accustomed to being the one cooking than the one sitting at the table, waiting to be served. The omelet is fluffy, stuffed with sausage and mushrooms. The coffee is darker and grittier than she's used to, the cream thick. Ash takes hers black. This time, Ro doesn't touch her fork until Ash has said the blessing and picked up her own utensils. They eat silently — Ash seems to prefer quiet while dining — and Ro regretfully stands to leave. She still has work, still has a life to live, even if she'd prefer to stay here in this little bubble, with everything they need right here. For someone who has thus far dedicated her life to her studies and her career, this is groundbreaking.

"When can I see you again?" she asks.

Ash glances at the cat clock, looking pained. "I'm really only free Sunday afternoon through Wednesday. I do most of my work on Thursday and Friday to gear up for the markets. I have ten dozen cupcakes to bake, soap to cut and label, plants to pack."

"Need help?"

A small twitch of Ash's lips, an odd kind of smile. "Oh, no. I like to work alone. You don't want too many butts in the kitchen, my grandmother used to say."

Ro looks around the kitchen, which is nice but small. The fridge doesn't look like it could hold two dozen cupcakes, much less ten. "Do you bake in here?"

"I have an industrial kitchen in the barn. Lots of expensive equipment. Hence the lock. But thanks for offering. Will you come to the market on Saturday? Once I'm on the other side of this, maybe we could make plans."

Ro kisses her on the cheek. "I'd like that."

Ash watches her fondly, leaning against the door jamb as Ro gets in her car. Ash's truck is parked over to the side, the chickens pecking excitedly at something underneath the rear bumper. Ro smiles at the thought of Ash snatching the eggs from under the hens this morning. The omelet tasted so fresh, the sausage juicy and perfectly spiced.

Back home, Ro showers and dresses and tries to remember what's happening in the real world. Her time with Ash is quickly overshadowing all else. A few weeks ago, this job was her point of pride and excitement, the beginning of her ambitions and a satisfying career she's been dreaming of since she got her first library card. Now it's just...this thing she has to do every day. This thing that keeps her from being with Ash. Even working on her next book doesn't hold the same obsessive appeal. It's hard to concentrate. She only wants to think about one thing.

She decides she wants to do something nice for Ash, surprise her while she's working. Of course, the trouble with dating — is this dating? — someone like Ash, someone utterly self-sufficient, is that Ash already does everything for herself. Ro can't cook better and Ash hates takeout and restaurants. Any flowers she buys won't be as beautiful as the ones Ash grows. She can't put together a self-care basket because Ash makes her own soap and lotion and salts.

But there is one way she knows to show affection.

After she has spent two hours trying to teach freshmen about symbolism while she daydreams about another girl's lips, Ro heads for the used bookstore downtown. She isn't certain what she's looking for until she finds it. An old book, thinner than a child's coloring book, but full of exactly what she's feeling.

The Love of Tiger Flower.

It's perfect.

Each page shines with beautiful illustrations and poetry about a tiger who falls in love with a flower.

Ro sees Ash as a cat, sleek and aloof and knowing, and herself as a flower just beginning to bloom.

She pays a little extra to have the book wrapped in brown paper, tied with twine and a dried poppy head.

On the way out to Ash's house, she is…well, nervous. She's never been here when not invited. It occurs to her that she invited Ash to her house, and Ash didn't so much turn her down as change the plans back to her place. Ro is a little put out. Not because hers is a better sort of house to be in — it's not — but because Ash has shared this intimate part of her life, and Ro would hope that Ash would want to be part of her world, too. Perhaps she can look for some local art at the next market, at least buy a painting and some flowers to spruce things up and make her place more personable. She can't cook like Ash can, but she has a great recipe for pizza dough, and they could make their own pizzas. Surely Ash likes pizza? Everyone likes pizza. She finds herself wanting to impress Ash, to please her. But isn't that how a relationship should be?

Her nerves jitter and jangle as her car bumps down Ash's long drive, past the fields and trees to what's beginning to feel like a secret world. Ash's truck is here, which is good. Gift in hand, self-conscious of her plain teaching garb, Ro knocks on the door, but there is no answer.

Well, why would there be? Ash told her she'd be working out back.

The stone path around the side of the house is familiar now. The terrible smell by the trash cans has dissipated, so it must be garbage day. There is a strange sort of scent in the air, though — something metallic and burning. Ro hopes Ash hasn't burned her cupcakes, as that would put anyone in a bad mood. Then again, she can't imagine Ash ruining food. She's too precise, too focused. Not like Ro, who can pick up a book and wander away from a pot of spaghetti and forget it exists until it's nearly boiled dry.

That haunting violin wafts out of the garden shed, and she reminds herself to check her snake plants soon. She's losing track of time; when is she supposed to dunk them? She's doing a very good job of neglecting them, that's for sure.

Chickens watch her curiously as she heads for the barn. The padlock is open, the door cracked a scant few inches. Whatever the bad, metallic smell was, it's closer to the house. Out here by the barn, she smells only the dreamy scents of vanilla and chocolate. Maybe the bad odor has something to do with making soap or candles, or maybe Ash is cleaning her kitchen oven while she's out here working so she won't have to smell it.

"Ash?" she calls, so she won't surprise her and make her spill a bowl of cake mix or ruin something even worse.

After a few moments, Ash appears in the barn door, squeezing out and standing with her back against the padlock. She's wearing old, stained, ill-fitting jeans and an oversized T-shirt with her hair in a hair net. She…does not look like Ash. She does not look pretty, much less pleased to see Ro, and Ro's heart shrinks three sizes.

"I told you I have to work," Ash says, voice flat and cold, with nothing close to a smile.

"I brought you a gift," Ro says, feeling very small and realizing she has somehow made a huge mistake. "I was thinking about you today, and…" She shoves the package into Ash's reticent hands. "I'm sorry. I'll see you Saturday."

Fighting tears, she scurries back up the path.

Right as she reaches her car, she hears boots on the gravel. "Wait."

Ro turns, knowing full well her eyes are wet and red.

Ash stands there, that little V between her brows, her hands in fists like she doesn't know what to do — a very unusual look for her. The paper-wrapped book is noticeably missing. "I'm sorry. You don't need to cry. When I'm working, I'm in a very specific mode. I don't want to be interrupted. This is just how I am. That's why I told you I wasn't available. I'm not — emotionally available, either. My work is important to me."

"I see that," Ro says carefully. "I guess I thought I would saunter up to find you in an apron, dancing around to boy bands as you frosted cupcakes. There's a lot to your work that I don't know. I see now that was assumptive of me."

"I need to set boundaries, and I need to know they won't be crossed, or this won't work." Ash looks down, kicks at the gravel. "It's a problem I have in relationships. People don't respect my privacy and time, so I have to end it."

Ro nods. "Okay. I can work with that. Just to be clear, you're not mad at me personally, but at the interference with your work?"

Ash exhales in relief. "That exactly. I'm not mad at you. I'm mad at the situation, and I want to make sure it won't happen again. So let me be clear: when I'm at work, don't call me, don't come here. Just respect my time."

Ro sniffles and nods again. "Lesson learned." Then she has an idea. "Can I send you letters, at least? Since you don't text or have email. Then I could say what I need to say and get it out of my system."

At that, Ash beams, and it's like the sun breaking through storm clouds. "I'd like that. Wait! Stay here. Don't move. I think I have a gift for you, too."

She hurries into the house, galloping like a colt. Ro feels like this is a small test, and thus she does not move, not so much as an inch. When Ash appears at the front door, she's carrying the sky-blue typewriter Ro noticed on a shelf.

"Think you could use this for your letters?" Ash asks.

Ro takes it with reverence and inspects the perfect keys. She doesn't know much about typewriters, but it looks like something from the sixties, maybe — kind of mod. There used to be a college guy who brought a little table downtown with a typewriter like this one — same color, even, although she never saw it up close — and offered to write freeform poems for five bucks. She envied his typewriter, back then, and this really does feel like a perfect gift. "If it's in good condition. I don't know how to replace ribbons or anything. And I wouldn't want to damage it."

"It's made of sturdier stuff than you think. Just put in a piece of paper and type. You can't hurt it."

Ro thinks about last night and feels her smile curl in. "You know, James Joyce used to write love letters to his wife, Nora. They were absolutely filthy. We tend to think of the past as prim and prudish, but they were up to a lot of absolute fuckery back then."

Ash's grin curls in to match. "Then write to me of absolute fuckery." She grabs Ro by the shoulders and kisses her on the forehead, and Ro smells that same burnt-metal odor in her hair. "Such a genius with words. Now go and let me work. Time is of the essence."

"Thank you. Sorry. I will. I love — " She stops herself. Where the hell did that come from? "This typewriter," she finishes awkwardly, which is true.

"I love that typewriter, too," Ash says with a smirk. She waves and heads back toward the barn.

As Ro drives home, she contemplates how she almost told someone she's been dating — if this is dating — for less than a week that she loves her. Yes, this is infatuation, but it feels like the relationship is progressing faster than usual, possibly because they're communicating so effectively. With men, Ro struggles to understand what they want in the moment and long term, if they're telling her the truth or just what they think she wants to hear. But with Ash, they just seem to *get* each other. Well, except when she missteps and makes Ash mad, but they fix that quickly without all the uneasiness and passive aggression she's fought in past relationships. With Erik, this would have been a full-blown fight — one that Ro would have automatically lost just because when she's emotional, she can't speak without her voice catching and shaking. That conversation she and Ash just had was A-level emotional work.

Ash may be aloof and private, but she is open and giving and forthright in a way that makes it seem like they've been dating for a year. There's a level of emotional trust that usually takes time and shared experience to build, but it feels like they've already reached a beautiful plateau. Every time Ro feels pushed away, Ash reaches out and pulls her back in.

That night, Ro sits down at her kitchen table and slides a crisp sheet of paper into the typewriter. She was so excited when Ash gave her this gift, but now there's a sense of expectation that brings only doubt. If she wrote all of what was in her heart, it would be too much. If she writes too little, it will appear as if she doesn't care. She offered absolute fuckery, but she can't bring herself to put her newly debauched thoughts on the page.

The thing Ash doesn't know yet is that while Ro is a gifted scholar and teacher of literature, she is not herself a storyteller. The words come to her when speaking but not when typing. Sure, her research-driven non-fiction is good enough to see print from a college press, but she's tried to write a novel at least a dozen times and can never decide where the story should start or even which stories are worth writing. It always feels to her as if there is some elusive perfect story out there waiting to be written, and that if she were meant to write it, the words would fall into her head as if whispered by the muse.

"I am empty of fuckery," she tells the typewriter.

As if in answer, her phone rings, and she looks down.

It's Ash.

She gasps and clears her throat before answering breezily.

"Have you written me a letter yet?" Ash asks. Over the phone, her voice is husky — or maybe she's thinking about the same thing James Joyce and his wife used to think about...

minus all the farting, because James Joyce was a weird little dude.

"I'm cogitating," Ro allows.

A soft chuckle. "Then let me give you something to write about. Do you have a bath tub?"

"Yes…"

"Light some candles and draw yourself a bath. Play music that relaxes you. Think of me. And…"

She describes what she wants Ro to do, and Ro's entire body shivers.

"Then write about it. Can you do that?"

"Yes…"

"Good."

Ash hangs up.

Ro knows what to do now.

Two hours later, the damp hairs curling up the back of her neck, her entire body heavy and wet and soft, Ro sits at the table in her robe, and the words find her as if falling from heaven.

> *The steam was high*
> *The water was low*
> *I made an archipelago*
> *Thinking of you*
> *Alone in the night*
> *Volcanoes erupting by candlelight.*

The typewriter keys are smooth under her prune-soft fingertips, and the insistent stamp of each inked pad on the stark white paper has a definitive sensuality about it. *Here is a letter,* that noise says, *and it cannot be undone.*

But instead of putting her missive in the mail, she drives all the way over to leave it in Ash's mailbox early the next morning. She doesn't want to wait any longer, doesn't want to wait two days for the post office to pull its head out of its ass. If she can't talk to Ash, she will give Ash her words as directly as possible.

When she opens Ash's mailbox, yesterday's mail is still there. Ro knows not to snoop, so she doesn't snoop, not really, but she can't help noticing that everything is addressed to the same person.

Elizabeth Gund.

She is about to put her letter in the box, but — no.

Something stops her.

Some strange instinct she can't name. Because if she puts the unstamped letter in the box, Ash will notice that it was placed there by Ro instead of the mail carrier, and she will know that Ro has seen a name that is not hers on all her mail.

Instead, Ro takes her missive back home, stamps it, and leaves it in her own mailbox to be picked up later and delivered as expected. She is following Ash's rule, respecting her boundary. Why did she even try to do something different? She should know by now not to do that. And yet, after Erik, she can't stop herself. She was afraid she'd find someone else's mail, and she did.

She googles Elizabeth Gund.

The only hits that come up are for a ballerina in the 1970s, a beautiful and gifted young star who faded out too soon and left her company due to an injury. As Ro scrolls through the few available images and sees one that's immediately familiar, it all comes together.

This is the woman from the photograph in Ash's childhood bedroom. This is *the* photograph in Ash's childhood bedroom.

Her grandmother was a ballerina.

Ro tucks that away for later but resolves not to ask Ash about it. If Ash wants her to know, she'll tell her.

She googles Ash Gund. Ashley Gund. Ashleigh Gund. Ashby Gund. Asher Gund.

Nothing.

Nothing on Google, nothing on Facebook, nothing on Twitter or Instagram.

Even if someone doesn't use technology, they should exist on the internet. And yet Ash does not.

Only now does Ro realize she has slept with a woman with no last name, a woman who doesn't seem to exist.

14

Friday is, again, endless. Ro's job used to be her entire world, but her gravity has shifted. She misses Ash with a physical ache, as if there is a long, long rope tying them together, a hook tugging at her ribcage. She does everything she's supposed to do, bathes and eats and takes notes for her book and goes to campus and grades papers and lectures on Dorian Gray and sits at her aged buffalo of a desk, staring out the window while counting down the minutes until office hours are over.

On Friday night she goes through an exacting list of ablutions, shaving and washing her hair and painting her nails rose pink. She wonders what will happen when Ash receives her letter. Will she like it? Will she write back? Will she read *The Love of Tiger Flower*? Will it speak to her as it speaks to Ro? Why hasn't she called? It might be nice to talk on the phone, and Ro can imagine Ash lying on her back on the floor, one long, elegant foot over her knee, her hair splayed out across the old wood boards as she twirls the phone cord around a finger. But that doesn't happen.

Ash said she was serious about her work, and she meant it. Ro wonders if, as time goes by, she'll be welcomed into that world.

What would it be like, to move in with Ash and wake up to feed the chickens and hunt for eggs with Anon twining around her bare ankles? How would it feel to see her clothes hanging in the closet beside Ash's pastel dresses, her shoes lined up with Ash's boots? She imagines there would be a pleasant feeling of companionship, a sense of completeness. Not the uneven partnership of a man and a woman who fit together like two puzzle pieces, but instead two vines twining together, reaching for the sun. Ash mixes up the metaphors in Ro's head, envelops her thoughts until Ro finds herself struggling for the right word. She is obsessed, she is compelled, she is called. She is a selkie, and Ash has her skin. It's infuriating and delicious and easy and challenging and tumultuous and she is hungry for more.

On Saturday morning she's nervous as a racehorse, pacing, waiting for the earliest possible time to leave for the farmers' market without looking as desperate as she feels. She's wearing a new dress, a breezy linen maxi with spaghetti straps that make her think of Ash's fingertips drifting over her shoulders. As she walks in from the parking lot, her jute bag empty, the world is a blur around her. Surely she passes other stalls and the food trucks, fussy children and angry mothers and badly behaved labradoodles, but she has tunnel vision. She barely breathes until she reaches Ash's stall.

Oh.

Ash is talking to a guy — a man, really. Forties, handsome, fit, put together in a way most men aren't. Ash is beaming — as in, she's literally glowing like a beam of light in her pink dress with her hair up in a ribbon crown. She laughs at something the man says and puts a hand on his forearm. Jealousy flares like dragon fire in Ro's chest.

She pulls back her shoulders, raises her chin, and moves forward confidently with a smile. She read somewhere once that if you walked through life like you were shooting lasers out of your breasts, you would exude power. She wants to incinerate this man on the spot, pew-pew-pew.

"Ash!" she calls, letting her excitement and affection burst out like a mustang that wants to run. She hurries over…

Until Ash gives her

A look.

A look that suggests this is her worst trespass yet.

If Ro's confident walk involved lasers, Ash's death glare is an atom bomb.

This is…similar to the look she gave Jessie.

Ro stops in her tracks.

"I just need to help this gentleman and then I can help you, miss," Ash says with careful, controlled professionalism.

"Oh. Okay." Despite herself, Ro is crushed. This is what puppies must feel like when they get swatted on the nose with a newspaper. She busies herself with the plant display, noticing a shelf of handmade pots she hasn't seen before, all white with a doily pattern imprinted in the clay. She picks one up and sees the same Ash Apothecary stamp on the bottom that she's noticed on Ash's soaps. Is there anything Ash can't do?

Well, except politely and warmly greet her…

Whatever Ro is to her.

She would have said girlfriend before today, but now she's not so sure.

The market is busy and loud this morning, with a mariachi band playing somewhere, so Ro can't hear much of Ash's conversation with the guy, as much as she'd like to. She only hears them laughing together, and her first thought is that they're laughing about her the same way she and Ash once laughed about Jessie. Is that what she is now, in public — some pathetic loser that Ash wants nothing to do with? Is there something about her that's embarrassing? Her cheeks burn hot, Ash barks a laugh, and Ro accidentally drops the pot.

Crash.

The look Ash gives her is the incarnation of fury, the glare of Medusa, and Ro is reduced to red-faced rubble.

"I'll pay for that," she says weakly.

"It looks like you've got your hands full," the man says. "We'll talk soon."

He leaves, and Ro squats to pick up the chunks of ceramic. She shoves them in her bag and pulls out a twenty. She didn't check how much the pot cost, but she needs to get out of here, now, before something worse happens — not that she can imagine something worse.

"Rosemary — " Ash starts, sounding exhausted and done.

"No. I'm sorry. I'll go. Is twenty enough? I didn't — "

"Rosemary, stop." Ash grabs Ro's hands, holding them firmly. "You've got to stop pitching a fit."

Ro's jaw drops, her nostrils flaring as anger quickly follows her shame. "Pitching a fit? You said I could come see you today, and then you treated me like an annoyance in front of that rando. Like I was some...some simpering sycophant! Like Jessie. Who was that guy, Ash? Why's he so special?"

Ash's head jerks back like Ro slapped her. "He owns the boutique hotel downtown and wants to carry my products in his guest rooms. So he's a big potential customer. Not that it's any of your business who I talk to."

Ro steps back, needing space. Ash isn't big, and yet she's so angry she's eclipsing everything.

"I guess it's not my business. I thought we..." She shakes her head. "Seems like it doesn't matter what I thought." She looks up, knowing full well she can't hold back her tears much longer. "Are you ashamed of me?"

Ash rolls her eyes. "It's not that simple. This is my job. This is my only source of income. Can you imagine if I walked into your classroom in the middle of a lecture and started batting my eyes at you in front of your boss? That's what you just did."

"You told me to come here," Ro says softly. "I was just excited to see you. That's not a crime."

"I would just expect you to be able to control yourself in public."

"Okay," Ro says. "Okay. I won't trouble you again." It's an interesting moment, in which she is suddenly and surprisingly losing something she'd thought was rock solid. Not because she doesn't want Ash — she does — but because she refuses to be treated this way, to be made to feel lesser. She may be infatuated, but she does have some self-respect. She has limits. "But tell me this: what's your last name? Is it Gund?"

Ash goes bone white and still as a statue. "Where did you hear that name?"

"You tell me and I'll tell you. Quid pro quo."

Ash just shakes her head in disappointment. "I never promised you answers."

Ro chuckles ruefully. "Ah, yes. The forbidden question in every relationship. Thou shalt not know thy lover's last name. You understand that's crazy, right? Okay. Well, it was transformative until you made me feel like shit. Bye."

She impotently tosses the twenty at Ash and hurries away. Ash calls out to her once, softly, but does not pursue her. Of course not. Ash isn't going to abandon her stall to chase after a histrionic ex-lover at the farmers' market. She's not going to make a scene.

The tears are flowing as Ro stumbles through the crowd. The scent of barbecue makes her stomach turn just now. In her car, she pulls a wad of fast-food napkins out of the glove box and mops off her face, but she would appear to be an endless font. The world is a blur as she drives home and unlocks her front door. She wants to beat the typewriter with a baseball bat, but she knows she would regret that one day. Maybe what happened with Ash was a mistake, but an antique typewriter transcends a bad breakup. Instead, she pulls out the remains of the ceramic planter and lays them out on the table. She picks up a small, sharp shard and presses the corner of it into her thumb until a bead of blood builds. She just needs to feel pain that isn't from Ash.

The pain brings her back to herself.

She's outside of it looking in, a third-person perspective on her life. So she got infatuated with an emotionally unavailable stranger. She fell in love with a beautiful mystery. This is no surprise; she's a scholar of literature, after all, and what is literature but the world's collective suffering writ large? Ash is — was — striking, unusual, mesmerizing, poetic, passionate, sensual. She was also confusing, stubborn, needlessly private, easily angered, a playground built over a minefield. Ro doesn't need that kind of thundercloud hovering over her life. She needs stability, friendliness, ease. If she wanted to spend time with someone who loves her but takes everything she says the wrong way and gets mad at her over stupid, useless things, she'd call her mom more often.

Back to her senses, she turns the piece of ceramic over in her hands, inspecting the strange texture of it. She took a few clay classes in high school, so she knows this was hand built and that Ash pressed a doily into the wet clay for texture. She can see the joins in the clay, the line where the glaze stops at the bottom edge, the hole in the base so the plant won't get waterlogged.

It's odd, though. When she looks at the broken edge, the clay isn't uniform. There are little white chunks in it, along with gray and black specks. Ro has never seen clay like this before. On a whim, she gets out the super glue and glues the pot back together. It's in several big pieces, and they fit neatly, leaving fine lines where the breaks occurred. The symbolism is fitting, Ro thinks. Kintsugi without the gold. Maybe when it's completely dry, she'll repot her snake plant in here. Tybalt and Romeo are thriving, after all. Maybe Ash was right — maybe she needs to be a bit more neglectful instead of lavishing the things she cares for with attention. She never did have any chill.

※

Ro pushes her way through the next few days like an icebreaker plowing through frozen seas. It's difficult and painful, and she feels cold and numb, but she keeps going, anyway. It's easy to teach *Gatsby* when all is lost. The party is over, and now someone has to do the tidying up.

Whether because her mind is a hamster on a treadmill or because she's drinking too much coffee just to function, she's having trouble sleeping. Anon isn't helping — he keeps yowling at the sliding glass doors, battering them with his paws at midnight, his fur puffed up. The first time it happens, Ro checks all the locks, but then it's every night and she tells her cat he's a beautiful little fool and locks him in her bedroom.

She dives back into writing her book, changing the premise slightly to focus less on feminism and more on betrayal. She makes her pizza dough and crams herself full of cheese and pepperoni, but it only makes her think of how much better it would be with Ash's homemade charcuterie. She takes one long, hot bath but understands she will never slip under the steaming water again without thinking of a blindfold and the touch of Ash's fingers. She buys a pink can of pepper spray and goes for a hike but sees the creepy guy's car still sitting there, now with a bright orange sticker from the police warning the owner that it will soon be towed. She wonders how he got home.

At the very least, he doesn't appear to own a spare set of keys. Ro smiles despite herself. It was beautiful, what Ash did to him.

Without Saturday morning at the farmers' market to look forward to, Ro's life loses its focus. She's not really looking forward to anything, but she's still searching for something. She goes to a faculty mixer and the grad students' wine bar and joins a book club but doesn't meet anyone who invokes even the tiniest bit of curiosity, much less excitement. She's back to feeling like the flaneur in a Manet painting, the person always outside the party. Ash may be strange and impossible, but she brought a rare thrill into Ro's life, and Ro is beginning to worry she'll never feel that giddy fizz again. At least she's getting lots of work done.

And then, on Tuesday night, her phone rings.

Ash's name pops up.

Ro stares at the phone like it's a snake and she can't figure out if it's venomous or not.

"Hello?" she finally says, more breathless than she'd prefer to sound.

"I'm sorry."

The words hang there between them. Ash sounds worn and agonized, like she's just walked across a desert and is desperate for a drink.

"Okay…"

"I've been keeping you at a distance all along. I'm scared to let anyone in. Scared to give anyone the power to hurt me. I set up unreasonable boundaries and get upset when you break them. You haven't done anything wrong. I'm just…I'm not that great with people sometimes. Being raised in isolation by your strict grandmother will do that. But I miss you. The market's no fun if I'm not waiting to see you. My days off are long and boring. I accidentally made a cheese plate for two, like you might just show up out of nowhere."

"You explicitly warned me not to do that."

A sigh. "I know."

"People in a relationship are allowed to show they care, Ash. To be respectfully spontaneous. That's…just how it works."

"Are we…in a relationship?" The hope in Ash's voice cracks Ro's heart wide open.

"We were. We could be. But I don't like feeling this way, like I'm being punished for something perfectly normal, something other people might even like. Bringing you a gift, being happy to see you — it shouldn't leave me skulking in a corner. I can't live my life walking on eggshells. You have to let me in."

For a long moment, Ash just breathes. Ro likes that she takes things seriously, at least.

"I'll try. But…it works both ways. I'll let you in, but that doesn't mean there are no boundaries. There are always boundaries."

"We might have to hammer those out, then," Ro admits. "To make sure we're on the same page. I can't respect a boundary that isn't obvious or that hasn't been clearly drawn. What happened Saturday destroyed me."

"I shouldn't have spoken to you like that, I know."

"I glued your pot back together. I put Tybalt in it. He looks fetching. I haven't killed him yet."

There's a long pause. No one is sure how to move forward.

"I liked your poem," Ash says in a small voice. "I thought you only did non-fiction. I missed you so much I even read your book — the one you sent, and then the one you wrote. I didn't know you were a poet."

Ro flushes with pleasure at that — Ash read her book! "I've never written poetry before now. You brought that out in me."

A pause. "Will you do something for me, Rosemary? Please?"

Now Ro is breathless.

"What?"

"Write me another poem and bring it over here right now."

Ro swallows hard, tearing up. "I can do that."

"I'll be waiting."

Ro is filled with a new energy, like she's been wearing concrete shoes ever since she walked out of Ash's life. But now she's a hummingbird, she's weightless, she's floating. She's forgotten every dark thought she's had this week. She's in pajamas, but she takes a quick shower and puts on jeans and a breezy button-up tank and fluffs her hair and does her eyes, all the while thinking of what kind of poem could encompass all that she's feeling just now.

She sits at the typewriter, knees jiggling nervously, but nothing bubbles up. Poetry is for long moments, sad moments, bittersweet moments, slow and sensual nights alone. Poetry fills an emptiness. Poetry doesn't happen when it's the only thing stopping a heart from flying miles away and closing the distance. Poetry should be an outgrowth, not a hindrance.

If only she could show Ash —

Wait.

Ro knows what to do. She takes care of the poem issue, grabs a bottle of Prosecco, and speeds down the country lanes. The sky is starless — a storm is rolling in. Ro feels the electricity moving under her skin. Perhaps she told herself she could live without Ash, but that doesn't mean she wants to. Every writer, after all, needs a muse.

15

When Ro arrives, the porch is lit with candles and a board of cheese and meat and fruit is waiting on the table, along with four cupcakes on a plate. Maple bacon, she thinks with a grin. Before she can step on the porch, Ash appears in the door holding a tray with two bubbling drinks. She puts down the tray and fidgets, which is unusual for her. Her grin is hopeful, radiant, pure.

Ro forgets every unkind thought she ever had about this girl.

They can make it work.

"I'm glad you came," Ash says. "I'm sorry — "

Ro runs up and dives into her arms, pressing her face into Ash's neck. Ash seems surprised at first, as if hugging is unusual, but then her arms come up and envelop Ro, and she puts her cheek against Ro's forehead.

"I'm all about moving forward," Ro says into the graceful curve of her throat. "If we can do that with openness, honesty, and understanding, then maybe we can stop saying we're sorry."

"But — "

Ro catches the back of Ash's head and gently pulls her in for a kiss. It begins soft and tentative and builds to something more promising, a call that Ash is more than willing to answer.

When they break apart, breathless, they're both smiling.

Ash takes her hand, leads her to the porch swing. "New crop of strawberries," she says. "And the tomatoes are good. Wasn't sure if you like them." There is indeed a side plate with ripe red slices of juicy tomato sprinkled with salt, but Ro hates tomatoes.

"They're beautiful, but I abhor them, I'm afraid."

The V appears between Ash's eyebrows.

"I'll make up for it with the strawberries, I promise," Ro assures her. "I get to have boundaries, too. And my boundary is this: even if you grow the best tomatoes in the whole world, until they're in a sauce, I'm not going to eat them."

At first, she's worried that this newfound assertiveness isn't going to work, but then Ash sighs. "They are the best tomatoes in the whole world," she mutters.

They eat, and Ash asks Ro how her week at work went, and Ro asks what Saturday's special cupcake was, and Ash tells her the good news, that the boutique hotel guy sent over a contract to stock Ash's soaps in all his rooms.

"It's my biggest contract yet," Ash says. "I'll be able to reach more customers than ever before. They want a signature scent, peaches and cream, although I might add a dash of sage." She chuckles. "It's nice to have someone to share good news with."

As the cheese disappears, Ash cuts a cupcake into quarters. Ro takes a bite and her eyes roll back. She's going to gain weight if she stays with Ash, but she doesn't think Ash will mind. The way Ash worshipped her curves that night...

Well, overindulging tonight won't hurt, at least.

The bacon is salty and crisp, the maple just sweet enough, the cake soft and fluffy. As they finish the last of the strawberries, the clouds that have been threatening all night flicker with lightning, and thunder rumbles warningly.

"Let's get inside," Ash says with a grin that melts Ro to her toes.

They carry in the plates and platters and glasses and the half-empty bottle of Prosecco. Ash's house feels deliciously familiar, and Ro is glad to be back. She takes the bottle to the fridge and is startled at how much meat Ash has stored within, seemingly endless hams and loins wrapped in plastic.

Hearing the fridge door open, Ash glances over and sees Ro's confusion.

"Farm share," Ash says. "From the farm down the road. I need to know where my meat comes from. The freezer's full, too."

"That's cool," Ro says, because it is. "No wonder the bacon is so good."

Ash's smile is strangely proud. "I'm glad you liked it." She reaches past Ro and closes the fridge door. Now she stands before Ro, places her hands on the fridge, framing Ro's face. Trapped, Ro is able to enjoy the sight of Ash's bare arms, so graceful and yet so muscular. The fridge hums against Ro's back, and she feels suddenly coy even though they both know why she's here.

"I read the book," Ash whispers in Ro's ear, her breath hot and her lips brushing Ro's temple. "Are you the poppy, then? Am I to tickle you?" She drags her nose down Ro's neck and kisses that most tender hollow at the base of her throat.

"If you want to shake off my pollen…" Ro says roughly, knees weak as they exchange metaphors from a book no one has ever heard of.

"Where's the poem I asked for?" Ash asks, a dark demand simmering in her words.

Ro unbuttons the top button of her shirt, revealing the word *Touch*.

Ash grins like a tiger and takes over.

Another button.

Me.

Another button.

Or.

Ash keeps unbuttoning.

I.

Will.

Die.

Ro's shirt hangs open, completely undone, and Ash takes her hand and leads her down the hall. Her bedroom is lit with candles, as if she knew without a doubt exactly where the night would take them, the air warm and heavy with the scent of beeswax.

"I want to worship you," Ash says, laying Ro out on the bed, her shirt already spread open like wings.

"Then I'm ready for adulation."

A small, delighted chuckle. "Adulation," Ash murmurs. "That rolls off the tongue."

She begins undressing Ro with tenderness and lavish attention, and Ro closes her eyes and becomes a creature of pure sensation. Thunder cracks, shaking the house, and Ro feels an answering quiver deep in her belly. This is like coming home, she thinks.

And then she doesn't think again for quite some time.

At one point, she is pulled back into reality by Ash's voice in her ear.

"My name," she whispers, "is Ashlyn Gund."

Ro's heart cracks open wider.

The time apart hurt, but now it's helping. Ash is letting her in, trusting her. It seems like a small thing, but it's a big thing.

"Thank you," she whispers back.

They fall asleep entwined, Ro's head cradled against Ash's shoulder. She is sated and soft and satisfied, relaxed for the first time in days. Ash let her touch her, this time, let her taste her. It felt like a revelation. The way Ash shivered and gasped, her body taut as a bowstring, Ro wonders if this is something new for her, if there's some reason she prefers to give pleasure instead of accepting it. Ro is grateful that she was given this gift, loved the little mewling whimpers Ash made, the look of wild abandon on her face.

She realized a long time ago that men can't change, that it's a foolish girlfriend who thinks she can rehabilitate a misbehaving beau, but she's beginning to think that women are capable of growing beyond. Ash apologized. She's opening up. She's letting Ro in. Things are going to be different.

The rain cocoons the farmhouse in white noise, broken only by cracks of thunder, and lightning that flashes through the flowered curtains. Ro snuggles in and dreams about waking up here every day without questions, without worries, without shame, without doubt, living a life in which sunlight is always streaming through the farm windows and Ash is always happy to see her.

16

Ro jolts awake and sits up after the loudest crack of thunder she's ever heard in her life shakes the house. The room feels warm and sick and still, and she realizes it's because the ceiling fan isn't moving. She pads over to the bathroom, but the light won't turn on.

"It's the breaker," Ash murmurs. "Gets overloaded when it storms sometimes. I'll reset it in the morning. Come back to bed."

Ro climbs back under the covers, but with the electricity out, there's no way she'll be able to sleep. She's a hot sleeper, and the air is heavy and stale and reeks of sex. The temperature is creeping up despite the rain; it's the hottest part of summer. She hates a room with no air movement. Ash falls deeply asleep again, snoring softly, but Ro can't do anything but lie there being annoyed.

Easy enough. She'll get up and reset the breaker.

She slips out from under Ash's arm and picks up her phone, turning on the flashlight as soon as she's out of the room. She doesn't recall seeing a breaker in any obvious place, but this is an old farmhouse and it could be anywhere. She starts in the kitchen and hunts in every conceivable nook and cranny. She feels a little ping of concern when she opens the pantry, because even though they haven't yet discussed Ash's firm boundaries, she wants to respect them. Still, Ash said she would let Ro in, and poking around the house for an electrical breaker is a very normal thing to do when the power goes out on a summer night.

The breaker isn't in the kitchen, the living room, the coat closet, or the spare bedroom. She knows it's not in the hallway bathroom. She doesn't recall seeing it in Ash's room or bathroom. This isn't the sort of house where there's a convenient niche to hide something like that.

Which means it must be in the closet across from the bathroom.

Behind the forbidden door.

Ro pauses, her hand on the doorknob.

Is this going to ruin everything? Is it going to start another fight?

Surely not.

Surely Ash will understand.

That's the whole point of tonight's reconnection — Ash is going to be reasonable from now on, do what couples do. And Ro wants to make Ash comfortable by fixing the current problem. She is a thoughtful person by nature, and she wants to take care of Ash like Ash takes care of her. If this closet was truly meant to stay closed, Ash would have a lock on it, like the barn outside.

This isn't like digging through someone's bathroom cabinet or Facebook messages, looking for evidence of wrongdoing — she no longer thinks Ash has any interest in Jessie or anyone else. This is just something people have to do in old houses with ancient wiring. It's as normal and natural as plunging a stubborn toilet.

"This will be fine," Ro tells herself, and she turns the crystal doorknob.

Much to her surprise, it's not a closet at all.

It's a stairwell — down to a basement.

And if this wasn't such a happy, friendly house, it's the kind of stairwell that would make her nervous. It definitely doesn't have the cozy feeling of the upstairs rooms. The walls are dingy cream, unpainted for years and draped with cobwebs, and the stairs are bare wood, dotted with layers of stains. It looks like someone has slopped leaking cans of paint up and down, carried furniture that has put gouges in the wall, and generally not treated this as a public area. No wonder Ash didn't want her down here — Ash is a tidy, clean person, and if this stairwell is any indication, the basement is going to be embarrassingly messy.

Pointing her phone's flashlight to light the way, Ro hurries down the stairs, wanting to get out of here as quickly as possible. The stairs terminate in a dead end with a door to either side, and the good news is that she's found the breaker — it's right there, at the foot of the stairs, facing her. She won't even have to explore the rest of the basement, which she's guessing is full of broken rocking chairs, boxes of newspapers, and the pastel polyester church clothes of a dead generation rotting on rusting metal racks.

At the bottom of the stairs, she opens the green metal door to the breaker box and flips all the switches back on. Even through the pounding rain, she can hear the air conditioner jangle back to life. She turns to dart back upstairs, but —

Well, she's by nature a curious person, and she wants to know what's down here that makes Ash so jittery. With a guilty glance back up to the top of the stairs, she opens the door, reaches into the room on the left, and flips the light switch.

And — *Fuck*.

❦ 17 ❦

Ro is an intelligent woman, so she immediately knows what she's seeing. The puzzle pieces fall together with a mental snap that would be satisfying if she didn't understand the danger she's in.

This…is an abattoir.

The room is unfinished, with an ancient concrete floor wearing a century's worth of stains. Stark light bulbs hang from the exposed studs overhead, and the walls are the same dull gray as the floor. There are two full-size chest freezers and a rumbling old fridge, a big wood butcher counter, and an ancient metal table like they use for autopsies. The kind of bright lights some people use for sewing and quilting are arranged around this table, all their cords running off to a surge protector. A wide array of surgeon's tools wait on a smaller table beside it, while the butcher's table boasts the sort of instruments a Civil War doctor would have required — bone saws and hammers and knives like machetes — plus something akin to a big soldering iron. There's a drain in the floor, stained but clean. Worst of all, there's a familiar figure strapped down to a portable hospital bed.

The creepy phone guy from the river.

Well, most of him.

He's missing both legs at the thigh. The stumps are wrapped in snowy white gauze.

He's got duct tape over his mouth and is wearing an adult diaper, and Ro can smell the stale urine from across the room. An IV runs into his arm, which is held down by multiple straps at shoulder, elbow, and wrist. He looks unwell, his eyes sunken and his skin pale. Seeing her, he thrashes and makes whimpering noises.

Ro shakes her head and backs away, her hand over her mouth.

No.

No no no no no.

Why would Ash — The guy's a creep, but *why* —

Ro tiptoes to the room on the other side of the stairs, opens the door, flicks the light switch, and sees a different sort of work room. It's finished out, for one thing, with flawless white walls and linoleum floors. In one area, several large pots sit on two electric ranges beside shelves covered in chemicals and soap molds. A small kiln lurks on an unfinished pad of concrete in another corner, along with boxes of clay stacked against the wall and a slab roller. One whole wall holds soap in all stages of processing, from empty molds to full ones carefully marked with their cure dates. Then there are shelves for inventory stacked with finished soap, beeswax candles, and ceramic pots. A scarred round table in the center holds labels, gingham squares of fabric with pinked edges, ribbons, and the stamps that mark all of Ash's work. Another table holds an ancient sewing machine and bolts of fabric in familiar pastels. The juxtaposition of what appears to be a crafty entrepreneur's work room next to a psychopath's kill room is jarring.

Ro backs out of the room and turns off both light switches. Her heart is beating so fast she can't tell if it's a panic attack or a heart attack. She didn't see a door to the outside in either room or she would run away and hide. She's naked, she's barefoot, she doesn't have her keys, but she has her phone and she would sprint to the road and flag down the next car or show up on a neighbor's doorstep.

Anything to get away from what she's just seen, from what she now knows Ash to be.

All Ash's anger, her hiding, her evasiveness, her need for boundaries and secrecy. Ro always thought she must be battling childhood trauma from growing up with a strict grandmother and without either parent. She was patient with Ash, gave her the space she needed as well as she could.

But Ash didn't just have a few little weird peccadilloes around privacy.

Ash is a straight-up killer.

Ro fumbles with her phone, can't quite unlock it. When she gets to the call screen, she puts in 9-1-1 and hits the green button.

"Come on," she murmurs. "Come on come on come on."

But the phone doesn't ring.

There's no signal.

She has to get upstairs and outside. Are there really no bars, or is it just because she's underground, surrounded by concrete? She realizes that, other than that time she called Ash's landline from upstairs, she's never actually looked at her phone when she was over here. Her entire attention has always been focused on Ash. Because that's what Ash does — she subsumes.

Ro has to get upstairs, and that means Ro has to be very, very quiet.

Her only hope of escape is to get up these stairs and out the front door. She's pretty sure her keys are in her jeans, on the floor beside the bed in which Ash is sleeping. She doesn't know where Ash's keys are; there's no convenient and obvious key hook by the door. Ash takes pains to keep most of those mundane details hidden — Ro has never even seen her wallet.

Her bare foot lands on the first step, and she flinches as it creaks the tiniest bit. She wants to pound up the stairs, burst through the front door, and run, but she knows that even if Ash is a heavy sleeper, she would hear those terrified, panicked, heavy footsteps. Ro puts her foot on the second step, and —

"Rosemary?" Ash calls from overhead.

Ro freezes, covering her phone's flashlight with her hand.

She can't go up the stairs now.

She has to hide.

She backs off the bottom two stairs and shines her flashlight into the workroom.

There is nowhere to hide here. Everything is neat and tidy. There are no boxes, no armoires, no convenient beds to hide under.

Reluctantly, she moves over to the other room.

The bad room.

The creepy guy flinches away from her flashlight and then rocks in his bonds, whimper-screaming.

"Shut up," Ro whispers, "or she'll come down here."

The speed with which the guy goes silent tells Ro exactly how scared she needs to be just now.

She contemplates the chest freezer but remembers too many stories of kids dying in them, plus she suspects they're full of meat—and not the kind from the local farm share. If she thinks about that too hard, thinks about the unusually rich sausage in her omelet and the sweet bacon in her cupcakes and the delicate slices of perfect prosciutto she gorged on, she'll be sick. The only place she can see that might possibly hide her is a small space in a corner behind some big drums. This would be easier if she was a smaller person, but she isn't, so she scurries over there and tucks herself into a tiny little ball, her phone clutched tightly in her hand, her finger firmly tamped over the flashlight.

Overhead, a door creaks open.

"Rosemary?"

God, Ro hates that name.

She told Ash so the first time they met.

And yet Ash insisted on calling her that.

If Ash had been a man and had crossed her boundary that hard and that often, Ro would've considered it a red flag. But

Ash is just a girl, an ethereally beautiful girl in a snowy white dress who loves flowers and old-fashioned things, and so Ro told herself it was an affectation, a cute little pet name between them.

As Ash walks slowly down the stairs, Ro catalogues everything that pinged her danger senses that she wrote off or ignored.

Ash calls her Rosemary even though Ro told her she doesn't like that.

Ash gets mad at her for any public display of affection.

Ash beat that raccoon to death without a second thought.

Ash punishes Ro every time she shows normal human curiosity in a way that Ash finds threatening, whether it's opening a door — okay, yes, sure, to an abattoir — or asking her last name.

Ash pushed this guy to the ground and threw away his keys and phone — and apparently went back into the woods to kidnap and maim him.

Ash has no online footprint, doesn't seem to exist in that space at all. Maybe Ash isn't even her real name. How would Ro even know?

With an even sicker feeling, Ro thinks back to when she brought Ash a snail, and later on, when Ash insisted she eat the freshly made tapenade even though Ro hates tapenade. When she was throwing up, Ro saw those rubbery gray bits. Did Ash put the raw snail in her food? Did she do it to make her sick, or — why?

Why would you hurt someone you claim to care for?

"Rosemary, are you down here?" Ash calls from the stairs, her voice low and wary.

Ro suddenly realizes that she's in a room full of weapons and yet has so far completely neglected to grab one. She is naked and defenseless, and she is being hunted by someone well versed in doing harm.

She has never felt like such an idiot.

Whatever Ash is, Ro fell for it.

She fell for a beautiful monster.

And considering she once wrote a term paper comparing the abusive relationship of Edward and Bella in *Twilight* to Heathcliff and Catherine in *Wuthering Heights*, she should have seen this coming. But she was blinded with infatuation like an absolute idiot.

And Ash preyed on that. She fed it like a farmer stuffing a veal calf.

The light clicks on, and Ro hunches down even farther. If Ash comes in this direction, she will be seen. The concrete floor is cold beneath the bare skin of her ass. A spider crawls over her arm, and it takes everything she has not to move, not to breathe.

"Rosemary?" Ash calls.

But she stays in the doorway. Ro doesn't hear the soft fall of bare feet.

The light flicks off, bathing her in darkness, and Ro exhales silently and sags with relief.

"Rosemary?" Ash calls, this time into the work room.

Seconds pass, and then the steps creak as Ash walks upstairs, still calling her name.

As if Ro is just going to pop out and answer.

After the upstairs door opens and closes, Ro makes herself count slowly to one hundred before she stands, shakes out her legs, and grabs a big, sharp-looking knife off the butcher table. It gleams in the light of her phone flashlight, giving her the briefest flash of her own terrified face. The creepy guy whimpers and wiggles, begging for her help. If he had legs — if he could walk — she might let him go. As it stands — *ha ha, he can't, he can't stand because Ash cut off his legs! Oh, God. That's not funny. Is this shock? Is this what it feels like to really and truly understand what the antelope feels like when it faces the lion?* — he can't even get down to the floor by himself. Even if the gauze on his leg stumps is white, those wounds must still be very raw and new. Ro is definitely not going to try to escape while carrying him. If nothing else, the sound of the Velcro straps ripping open would immediately alert Ash to Ro's whereabouts.

"If I get out, I'll send someone back for you," she whispers.

His whimpering amplifies to frantic screaming behind the gag.

He doesn't think she'll be able to escape.

That…makes Ro think.

She was going to run up the stairs with the knife and hope Ash would be far enough away that she could get outside and out of sight. But watching this bigger, faster, stronger man — Ash's prey — shriek his fear and fury, Ro begins to think that won't work.

There must be a window or a door down here. There's got to be something. Knife in one hand and phone in the other, Ro checks every inch of the wall that would face the backyard. It's solid concrete with no breaks. She moves to the work room and realizes that there might be something behind one of the many sets of shelves. As Ash's footsteps creak overhead, hunting her,

Ro tries to silently inch the soap-supply shelf away from the wall and is disappointed to find yet more smooth, white-painted drywall. The soap-curing shelf is on the wrong side of the house, which means her last chance of escape without a fight is behind the clay shelf.

As she shuffles across the room in the darkness, she stubs her toe on something and swallows back a cry. When she points her flashlight down, she finds a cardboard box lined with plastic and filled with ashes.

No.

Not ashes.

Cremains.

She remembers what it looked like when her mom sprinkled her dad's ashes in his favorite lake, so she recognizes this particular texture, like cat litter with little white chips and black freckles. She's seen that same texture recently — in Ash's homemade pot.

Ro's eyes slide to the kiln.

Fuck.

The girl really doesn't let anything go to waste.

Ro shakes that off, puts her knife on the ground, and pries the shelf away from the wall. Lightning flashes through a narrow window, high up and mostly blocked by grass. If she can move the shelf, find some way to climb up there, and get it open, it's possible she can squeeze her way out, but it won't be fun.

None of this is fun.

So bizarre, so twisted, so surreal that a few hours ago she was as happy as she's ever been. She had a beautiful, sensual night with a killer. She fell asleep naked holding a hand that had recently sawed off a man's legs.

Wait.

All that fresh meat in the fridge.

It was *him*.

But before him, before Ash took his legs — *oh God, his legs!* — there were maple-bacon cupcakes and charcuterie and pork loin, and there's lard in the cupcake frosting and even the bread, Ro realizes now, and all that *soap*…

Her gorge rises.

How many people has Ash killed? How many different people has Ash…fed her?

Her stomach is currently full of —

Ro swallows it back down and focuses on the shelf. She has to get it away from the wall. She has to keep it upright, not jiggle anything on it, not let anything fall off or make a single sound. With her phone in her mouth, she grasps the wood.

At least it's not a terribly heavy shelf.

Inch by inch, the shelf angles away from the wall. She's sweating now, hates how aware she is that she's naked when she should be entirely focused on getting out of here. In the room across the stairs, the creepy man continues to whimper and scream and cry into his gag, rattling the bed as much as he can. Ro wonders if he's trying to get her caught or if he's just so far gone that he can't control himself anymore. Trapped in a basement, hooked up to tubes, staring at his own stumps, how long could anyone remain sane?

The shelf is finally far enough away from the wall that Ro

could conceivably slip outside. She picks up a chair from under the work table and carefully, silently places it under the window. The chair wobbles as she steps up and grabs the window ledge so she won't fall. Her phone almost slips out of her mouth, but she has no place to put it. It's almost comical, how at her most traumatic and needful moment, a woman still does not have pockets.

If she lives to tell the tale, she'll laugh about that one day.

The single catch on the window is rusted shut, and she fiddles and fidgets with it, barely getting it to budge. Finally it wrenches sideways with a rusty squeal that makes her flinch. She pushes the window open and rain flicks in as thunder rumbles. She pushes and pushes, but the window doesn't seem to want to open out all the way — it's the kind that swings up and out. There's something blocking it.

One of those beautiful clay sculptures.

Maybe if she pushes hard enough, it will fall over or break.

Before she goes that route, she holds up her phone, hoping for just one bar.

None appear.

She shoves the window, hard, and the sculpture topples over outside. The pane can move now, but it won't stay up on its own.

Why is this so goddamn hard? Why is crawling out of a window suddenly the most impossible thing in the world?

She needs something taller than the chair if she's going to get out.

She hops down and fetches a box of clay. It's heavier than it has any right to be, but it should give her just enough of a boost to get out the window. She puts it on the chair and carefully steps on it, feeling the clay within dent under her weight. She settles the phone gently between her teeth and pauses and acknowledges that this is going to hurt like hell but she has no other choice. With a deep breath, she boosts herself up, using every ounce of strength in her arms to get her torso through the narrow window, scraping her breasts and forehead, and —

"Hello, Rosemary."

Ro barely hears it over the rain and thunder outside.

Ash's cold, white, rain-wet foot presses against her forehead — a benediction — before firmly pushing her back inside.

⚛ 18 ⚛

Ro falls backward into the shelf, toppling it over and landing hard on it on her bare back. She scrambles to her feet in the absolute darkness, hunting for her phone. She must have pulled a muscle where her back meets her shoulder because she can barely move her neck, and a strange numb pain shoots down her arm as she feels around on the floor for the one thing that might still save her. She finally finds her phone, then uses its flashlight to find the knife.

The man in the other room is going crazy, screaming around his gag and shaking so wildly the hospital bed is rattling, and hard rain pelts the glass of the window that has fallen shut, and the door at the top of the stairs opens, and all Ro can do is aim her phone flashlight at the door, hold her knife, and get ready to fight, despite the fact that everything hurts and she can barely breathe and her heart is jackhammering in her throat.

Step. Step. Step.

Ash takes the stairs slowly, and Ro imagines she's enjoying this, that whatever she gets out of killing people, she's now excited by the thought of Ro's fear and helplessness. When Ash appears in the door and flicks on the overhead lights, her long white nightgown is soaking wet and plastered to her skin, her feet bare, her hair up in a messy bun. She looks like she just stepped out of an Instagram ad for cottagecore dresses... except for the fact that she, too, is holding a knife. And hers is bigger.

"All that talk of not crossing my boundaries..." she says with what seems like genuine sadness.

Ro's eyes bounce back and forth, an animal hunting for an egress. "The power was off. I just wanted to flip the breaker. I thought I was being helpful. It's a normal thing to do!"

"Not when you've been told explicitly not to go where the breaker is. I said I would let you in, and you went straight to the one place you were never meant to see."

"So put a lock on the fucking door!" Ro shouts. "Do literally anything to hide it!"

Ash steps toward her, leaving wet footprints on the linoleum. She plays with the tip of the knife, twisting it between her long fingers. "All you had to do was stay away from that door. Just one door. And you couldn't do it, Rosemary. You just... couldn't...stop yourself. It was a test — of your love, of your loyalty. I chose you because I thought you were a genius, and it turns out you're stupid, just like the rest of them. Like a sheep that is determined to die." She shakes her head. "I'm beginning to think every artistic genius is secretly an idiot."

Ro thinks back to all the flower paintings upstairs with their signatures chipped off. "How many geniuses have you met, Ash?"

Ash smirks and cocks her head. "Oh, you're going to try to stall me? That's fine. I still love you, even if you've ruined everything and broken my heart. *How many geniuses have I met.*" She holds up a finger.

"There was Serena. When her fingers moved over the violin strings, it vibrated my soul. She should've been in the symphony, but she had anxiety. Couldn't play in front of anyone. Except me."

She holds up a second finger. "Jewel, the sculptor. Taught me everything I know about clay and kilns. Her work almost seems alive, doesn't it? Like her creatures might run away into the garden if you snuck up too fast. I think you chipped that gnome when you forced open the window, Rosemary." She shakes her head. "Rude."

She holds up a third finger. "Then there was Shannon. He was a street poet. And a pervert. I decided men were too shallow to bother with, after that."

A sigh. "Then there was Milla. The painter. The way she used light and color was extraordinary. I used to call her my little bee, because it was like she could see on a spectrum the rest of us couldn't."

She holds up a fifth finger. "And my grandmother, Lizzy. My first genius. She was a ballerina, the greatest of her generation. But then her artistic director got her pregnant and kicked her out. Publicly, they said it was an injury, but really it was all for his convenience and reputation. It was the death of her art. She came back here to live with her parents, who grew even stricter and cut her off from pretty much everything. They'd never wanted her to dance, and she'd only proven them right. My great-grandparents died together in a barn fire." Ash's mouth twitches. "I often wonder if that was Lizzy's work but never had the guts to ask her. She was strong and wise…but cruel. By the time my mother had me and ran off, my grandmother had left dancing behind forever and reclaimed her roots here. She taught me everything I know."

With her eyes pinned to Ro, Ash steps to the soap shelf and pushes it back to where it belongs. "Maybe she began as a ballerina, but my grandmother's real genius was in survival. Scraping a life out of nothing. Using every ounce. Scraps feed the chickens. Eggs and bones and blood are fertilizer. Collect the slivers of soap to make new soap. Feed a broken chair to the fire. Turn an old dress into rags. Every ounce counts, she used to tell me. Waster, waster, turkey baster." Ash's face goes flat. "When she caught me throwing away something that could be reused, she used a turkey baster full of hot water on me. Guess where it went, Rosemary. Can you guess? I learned my lesson." She points with her knife to enunciate each word. "Don't. Waste. Anything."

The pieces are all falling into place, and Ro realizes that she was so bewitched, she missed a hundred red flags. She would have caught them in a man, but in a beautiful, harmless-looking girl like Ash?

She fell for it.

But Ash loves her, too. She can feel it. In whatever sick, twisted way this broken girl can love, she does. Ro has to tap back into that.

"You know, you don't have to hurt me," she says. "Look at it this way: I've already seen the thing you didn't want me to see. What if I can live with it? What if we can still be together?"

Ash snorts and rolls her eyes. "I know you, Rosemary. You may have flashes of genius, but you're not like me. You're not like *this*. When I killed that raccoon, it was a test. I thought you would run away. I hoped you would be curious, that it might spark something in you. But you were disgusted and too stupid to leave."

"Too ensorcelled to leave," Ro admits. "I loved you already, and I was willing to accept that part of you."

The V appears between Ash's brows. "Accept it? Like you're doing me a favor? Tolerating me? No, Rosemary. There are only two ways to be with me. Ignorant and trustworthy and well behaved, or by my side, of the same mind. And you can't do that. That's not who you are. So you'll end up where all the other failed geniuses end up."

"And where's that?" Ro asks softly, because she has to know.

Ash perks up. "You really want to hear this? Okay. Put down your knife and I'll tell you."

Ro considers it. Ash is between her and the door. Ash has a bigger knife that she has used on a human being before — many times. Ro has never hurt anyone worse than kneeing Stevie Holiday in the balls in kindergarten when he asked her to kiss his peenie. Ash is taller, faster, stronger, and motivated to make sure Ro never leaves this room. If she's going to get out alive, it has to be with her real weapon: words.

With a nod, with her eyes locked on Ash, she kneels and places her knife on the floor. And then she sits and draws her knees up to her chin, because her back hurts, and she can barely keep herself upright.

"I've never told anyone this before," Ash says, smiling fondly. "It's nice of you to ask. No one ever asks." She paces as she speaks, waving the knife around like a conductor's baton. "So, first I take the meat. In there, where David is. I parcel it out like pork, wrap up the loins and butts and make my salami and sausage and coppa and bacon and prosciutto. Or freeze it. I put the head in the kiln to get rid of teeth so they can't be used for dental records. It also takes care of the hair, bone, that sort of thing. I melt down the fat for my soap and cupcakes. Works just like lard, and people go crazy for it. What's left goes into the raised beds outside, which is why my tomatoes are so good — not that you'd know — although I do have to keep the raccoons out." She smiles proudly. "Everything gets used. Every little bit." She winks. "Even the liver."

Ro looks up from the floor, arms crossed over her chest, feeling like a little kid in kindergarten who just doesn't understand.

"But...why?"

Ash squats and lifts Ro's chin with the tip of her knife. "Because my grandmother always told me I was stupid. The stupidest little girl alive. She said she was a genius of infinite potential, and somehow she ended up stuck at home, raising a cretin. So when I got old enough, I decided that maybe I couldn't be a genius, but I could consume one. For someone who thought herself a genius, she was certainly taken by surprise. Very easy to kill. I was clumsy then, but it worked. It made me a better person. Made me *stronger*. So I kept doing it."

Ro is so very careful to keep her face neutral, to appear interested, but inside, her stomach is sour and turning. Based on this story and what Ash said when she talked in her sleep, Ro can now see that Ash grew up with extreme abuse, both emotional and physical, even sexual, and that it has broken her beyond all hope.

And yet…there is a part of her that loved Ash, that saw her as a ray of light in a dark world, as someone who sees behind the curtain, someone alive and vital and curious and interesting. That's what she has to show Ash now.

That's the only way Ro will make it out of here alive.

"There's a poetry in that," she says. "An equilibrium."

"Yes! Thank you!" The knife whips away from Ro's chin as Ash stands and paces again. "Do you really see it, Rosemary? Do you think you could try? *Will* you try?"

Ro looks up, confused. "Try?"

Ash's smile is hopeful, radiant, jubilant. "Come kill him with me. Let's do it together. Show me that you love me. Show me that you understand."

Ro swallows hard and nearly pees herself, naked on the linoleum floor.

Perhaps…she has played her part too well.

At least going to the other room will give her a chance to escape. Maybe she can find a way to get upstairs, even.

"Can I pee first?" she asks. "I — I need to go."

"Kill first, then pee." Ash reaches a hand down, and Ro takes it and winces as she's pulled to standing. "Did you hurt yourself?"

Ro nods. "My back, when I fell into the shelf."

Ash looks at the shelf, annoyed. "I hate it when things are messy down here. You're going to have to help me clean that up."

"I'd be glad to. I'm sorry. Just let me use the bathroom."

Ash walks to the doorway and stands. "Go on."

Ro exhales a shaky breath and hurries to the stairs. But when she tries to go up, Ash blocks her with the knife. "I already told you: kill first, then pee. Then clean up your mess. Then breakfast. For a creepy asshole, he tastes just fine. Chickens are like that, too. Their personalities don't affect the quality of the meat."

Ro has no choice but to go into the other room — the worse room.

"Turn on the light," Ash commands.

So Ro steps to the doorway and flicks the switch and glances at the table laden with knives and saws, so close and yet so far. Ash is watching her every move, she knows, and she's now in too much pain to fight back. The creepy guy — David — goes crazy. With just Ro, he was hopeful, eager, begging to be released. But with Ash, he closes his eyes, shrinks back, wails.

He has watched this woman saw off his own legs.

Ro would turn away, too.

Ash herds Ro over to where David is strapped to the hospital bed, always keeping herself between Ro and the door. Even in this moment of stunning terror, Ro's mind seeks the safety of books, and she imagines herself the last unicorn being driven into the sea by the Red Bull. Beside her, Ash places the blade of her knife against the man's exposed neck. With his head strapped down, he can't protect this most tender and vulnerable spot. Ro notices now that the bed is wrapped in thick plastic. The scent of urine strikes her nose again, but fresh this time. She can empathize with his fear.

"Rosemary," Ash murmurs, voice husky. "Give me your hand."

Like a child on the way to a spanking, Ro holds out her open hand, and Ash puts the knife handle in it and wraps it with both of her own. Ro feels the strength there, the tension. There is no world in which she turns this knife against the hand that sharpened it, and they both know it.

"Do you love me, Rosemary Katherine Dutton?" Ash asks.

Ro never told Ash her middle name, but she is no longer surprised by what Ash secretly knows.

"I love you, Ashlyn Gund," she replies, because this is the only possible reply.

In a split second, her hand firmly caught, Ro's brain runs a hundred different scenarios, a hundred different ways this could go. She cannot see a way out. She can see only one way to stay alive.

But is she capable of doing it?

And if she does it, is she capable of living with herself afterward?

She is. She has to be.

If she can live this lie long enough, then she'll find a way to escape.

"Are you ready?" Ash asks.

Ro licks her lips.

She is crossing the Rubicon.

What is about to happen cannot be undone.

"I'm ready."

With a slow, sensual slash, together, hand in hand, they slit David's throat.

19

It is a beautiful morning, and Rosemary sits on the porch with a perfect cup of coffee in one hand and a book in the other. Ash surprised her with the deluxe set of Jane Austen, the ones with the pretty pastel covers, and she's enjoying revisiting her old favorites. When she was teaching and writing her own books, she had to tear everything apart, dig down through the skin, past the muscle, to the very bones to expose meaning for her students and readers, but now that she's left her job, she can read for enjoyment again. Anon sleeps on the ground, his speckled belly fluttering as he purrs.

Ash appears in the door in the same long, lavender dress she was wearing the day Rosemary met her. "The muffins are finally ready," she says. "Cinnamon crunch."

"My favorite."

Ash brings out a tray and places it on the small table. There's a bowl of cut strawberries, a vase of gardenias, and two muffins, still steaming hot, with pats of fresh homemade butter melting inside.

"Thank you," Rosemary says. "You're always so thoughtful."

"It's easy to be thoughtful when you love someone," Ash tells her, dropping a kiss on her forehead before she heads back inside.

Ash has lots of work today. It's soap day. Rosemary tries to stay outside when the fat is melting downstairs. Maybe she can't taste it in the baked goods, but the smell of it simmering on the basement stove makes her sick to her stomach. Ash has no idea. Rosemary was once a theatre kid, an actress, and she has become very good at hiding how she feels.

She puts down the book and coffee and reaches for a muffin. It burns her fingertips, but she's too hungry to wait a second longer. She gobbles the top half of the muffin, cramming it in her mouth, swallowing to get it down.

The chickens charge up the porch steps and cavort around her, desperate for crumbs.

The greedy things will eat anything, she's learned: leftover cheese, rotten fruit, any kind of meat. They'll lick blood from the gravel if they find it. Rosemary is darkly amused that Ash has raised these chickens to eat human meat, and then they in turn eat the chickens. It's the circle of life. She can't let herself think about it too deeply. She has to keep up the charade.

After she's cleaned her plate — because Ash always prefers that she clean her plate — she tosses her muffin crumbs off the porch, sending the chickens into a frenzy, and realizes there's something under the plate. A magazine.

She perks up.

She knows what this is.

She's been waiting for it to arrive.

She didn't think Ash would let her submit her poetry anywhere, but she played on her vanity, reminding Ash that she had captured a genius and that geniuses must get their work out into the world somehow. The poem is anonymous, but if the magazine is here, then her poem made the cut.

She flips through the pages anxiously until she finds it.

Aftermath

By An Anonymous Scribe

One day I fell
Helpless in a heap
When I saw beauty so sweet
Unctuous, soft, and fair
I crave her like manna
I weep
I weep
Every time I breathe
I'm filled with need
The flow and ebb
Of my idolatry
Begins and ends in her eyes
My love is pale
Her hair a golden river
Before her, I knew only ennui
After, ever a soft sort of mania

In her presence, I fall
To my knees, to my back
She is she, and I am I
And together, we are ideal
Two halves of a moon so full
Even when eclipsed, it is complete
The chandler and the raconteur.

Rosemary reads it, then reads it again.

Ash can't have figured it out, or it wouldn't be here.

Ash wouldn't kiss her on the forehead if she'd discovered the hidden message in the last letter of every line.

Rosemary doesn't know what good it will do, considering the poem has been published anonymously, but perhaps with her next foray, she'll give the street name and city.

She spent forever on that poem, on getting the fifty-cent words just right to distract Ash out of reading too carefully, to woo her and stroke her ego. For all that she is crafty and clever, for all that she can make anything out of anything, Ash's Grandma Lizzy was right: she is not a genius. And maybe Ro isn't either, but she still holds out hope that she will one day find a way to escape.

"Did you find it?" Ash asks from the door, surprising her.

"Yes, but I didn't read it," Rosemary lies. "I'm always a little shy, to see my work in print."

Ash's bare feet squeak as she walks across the porch.

"You know, I didn't notice it before I sent it in for you," she says sweetly. "But once it's in print, it's hard to miss."

Rosemary's heart speeds up. "Miss what? Was there a typo?"

Ash stands before her holding the bone saw from the basement.

"Your little message."

Rosemary's hands clamp down on the arms of her chair, and she swallows hard. "What message?"

"Didn't you learn?" Ash asks. "Couldn't you just let it go? We're happy here, aren't we?"

"Ye — yes, of course," Rosemary says, too quick.

She can't take it anymore. She throws herself out of her wheelchair and falls on the floor, pain radiating up the stubs of her thighs, still sensitive even months after Ash tied her down and sawed off her legs so she couldn't ever leave.

Together, they crafted emails quitting Ro's job and telling her mother she was officially going no-contact. Ash wiped and threw away Ro's phone and cleaned out her little rental house, brought Anon and Tybalt and Romeo and the other things Ro needed back here and fixed the spare bedroom up to suit her. She attached rails beside the toilet and in the shower and bought the wheelchair. Outside of claiming Ro's legs and feeding them to her over many, many meals, Ash has been the perfect partner.

After all, Rosemary can no longer cross boundaries. She can't go down to the basement. She can't go anywhere. Ash made sure of that.

Ash kicks her over, puts a bare foot on her stomach as Rosemary squirms like a bug toward the porch steps.

"If you don't have hands, you can't type," Ash tells her.

"But I thought…I thought you loved me for my words!"

Ash straddles Ro's chest, sinks her knees onto her arms. Ro remembers the first time she saw that corn-silk hair, those ice-blue eyes, that constellation of freckles, those perfect, tiny teeth.

"You'll still have your tongue," Ash says. "For now."

And she grabs Rosemary's hand and pins it over her head and brings the bone saw down.

ACKNOWLEDGMENTS

This story was inspired by my daughter, who shares my love of the TV show *Hannibal* but asked why all the hot serial killers are always dudes.

I told her they don't have to be.

I'm grateful she asked.

And I'm grateful to Thomas Harris and Bryan Fuller for creating such captivating characters and beautiful visuals. I'm still waiting on Season 4.

I'd like to thank Cath Trechman and the team at Titan for believing in this story. Julia Lloyd has created one of the most beautiful covers of my career, and I simply cannot stop looking at it. I'd also like to thank Elora Hartway for pulling it all together and the publicity and marketing teams, particularly Katharine Carroll, Kabriya Coghlan and Hannah Scudamore.

Thanks to my ferocious agent, Stacia Decker, who cultivated *Bloom* with me until it had the presence of a blossoming Corpse Flower.

Thanks to Stephen Graham Jones, who offered encouragement and answers when I wasn't sure what to do with a book that was decidedly pint-sized.

Thanks to Eric LaRocca, who's been killing it in the horror novella world recently, giving us all newfound hope.

Thanks to everyone who read an early copy and offered such delicious quotes: Kristi DeMeester, Rachel Harrison, Gabino Iglesias, Gwendolyn Kiste, Eric LaRocca, Hailey Piper, Paul Tremblay, Chuck Wendig, and Ally Wilkes. And thanks to Kevin Hearne, who hasn't read it yet but is always in my corner.

Thanks, always, to my husband Craig, for introducing me to Ben Burton Park in Athens, back in the day.

And thanks to you, dear reader, for giving it a chance. I hope it sticks to your bones in the best possible way.

ABOUT THE AUTHOR

DELILAH S. DAWSON is the *New York Times* bestselling author of over twenty books and dozens of comics and short stories for all ages in multiple genres ranging from horror to fantasy to romance to well-known properties like *Star Wars*. She once worked in a haunted house and excelled as both a cannibal and a corpse. She lives in Atlanta with her family and loves fancy cupcakes made with gluten-free flour and other normal ingredients. Find her online at www.delilahsdawson.com and on most social media as @delilahsdawson.

For more fantastic fiction, author events,
exclusive excerpts, competitions, limited editions and more

VISIT OUR WEBSITE
titanbooks.com

LIKE US ON FACEBOOK
facebook.com/titanbooks

FOLLOW US ON TWITTER AND INSTAGRAM
@TitanBooks

EMAIL US
readerfeedback@titanemail.com